SOL & SIMONTON

TEDDY MCMILLAN

Published by QuestVersity, LLC

Visit our website at www.questversity.com

First published in 2020

ISBN: 978-164970926-4

Printed in the United States of America

Dedication

For those unforgettable moments when my mother took me to Alabama during the winter and summer, and I spent time in the woods with my cousin, Murdock.

I can still smell the warm fires glowing in the living room chimney and hear the crackling of the dry wood, and feel the butterflies dancing around in the pit of my stomach as we moved through the eerie woods on daily adventures on our grandparents' land.

*

To my number one fan, my Queen, my wife, Dominique. You inspire me daily and I couldn't ask for more in a friend and soulmate. I love you.

*

For my two beautiful princesses, Imani and Moon, and my prince, Sir Teddy. My love for you is infinite, surpassing the stars and transcending the universe. Only God can truly comprehend.

*

For my mama and daddy, who are no longer with me in the physical realm. I know you are with me in spirit. I miss you and will see you again.

*

To my brothers and sisters, who have looked out for me all of my life, I love you and thank you for everything you have done for me.

Other Books by Teddy McMillan

FICTION

Hi-Jinx Drama (coming in 2021)

Diamond Lane: A Fleetwood Mahone Story (15 year gold version - Coming in 2021)

The Faction: A Fleetwood Mahone Story (coming in 2021)

NON-FICTION

Five Eleven and a Half: A Nappy Headed Kid from Compton (coming in Fall 2020)

SOL & SIMONTON

CHAPTER ONE

1943 - Sumerville, Alabama

It's really hot. I weave in and out between tall hickory trees, pulling the wiry branches away from my body and moving through the dense woods. I follow the fresh footprints of my silly cow, and they lead me to the most dreadful place I can imagine. This place makes my heart pound like crazy, so fast that it nearly popped right out of my chest the last time I was here.

"Hey," a chilling voice blares, sending fluttering echoes in my head. I twitch and stand dead in my tracks like a statue. *God, please get this fool. I'm just a lil ole thirteen-year-old kid.*

I see the strain and tautness in the old, white man's face and his arms swing hard and fast as he storms at me. He makes an abrupt halt just a few feet away and points his long, crooked finger at me. His shoulders are broad, and the sun wraps around his frame with a harsh glow.

1

TEDDY MCMILLAN

I widen my eyes. He stands there like a complete idiot, just panting and pointing with his eyes locked in on me. I take two steps back and tilt my head so that I can see him clearly. His eyes pierce me through the thin-rimmed glasses with nothing but fury. Veins bulge through his forearms like slithering rattlesnakes, and his cheeks sag and his earlobes are like long narrow flapjacks connected to his reddened face. His chest pulsates in and out and I feel his rage intensify with every measured breath. *I bet his old snagga-tooth butt can't catch me if I run though.*

I feel a tightness around my eyes and my heart beats erratically like rhythmic thuds from a crazed drummer. I ease one foot back over the damp grass to position my body just enough for a quick escape. He finally gives his finger a break and rests his palms on his hips.

"That's the last time yo' animals gon' be on my property. I den told you and yo' mama more times than enough to keep yo' damn animals off my property." He scuffs the dirt with one of his worn boots. His bottom lip curls and he swings his arm at the fence. "That damn cow is on my property again. She den tore up the fence and made her way right over here and mixing in with my cattle. I have good reason to put a bullet in her head."

My hands tingle. I take short cautious steps toward the opening in the fence, never letting my eyes off this moron.

"Sir, I apologize, sir," I whisper, in the humblest tone that I can muster. "I'll take that ole cow back home right now. Just let me know where she is, and I'll go get her." The fence is raggedy in some parts. One of the round wooden posts is broken at the bottom, the barbed wire hangs loose at the end, and parts of the wire are matted into the mushy dirt from being trampled over.

"Where is she?" I ask, still feeling a bit jittery.

The old man's anger deepens. "She's exactly where I told you she is. She's on my land," he yells.

I extend an arm, push a palm at him, and give him a slight murmur, "Okay, sir." When I get closer to the post, I kneel and take a closer look at the opening in the fence. I squint at the small animal tracks embedded in the dirt.

"Whatchu lookin' at?" he says, in an abrasive tone.

"Nothing, sir. Just looks like the same thing that happened to the other side of the line down yonder. Me and my mama been tryna handle them wild boars that's been tearing up everything. They came in and killed like four of our chickens already and ripped some of the boards clean off our barn." The man clears his throat. *Why is he still lookin' stupid?*

"Wild boars? Ain't no wild boars den came through that fence there. That's that same ole cow that came through there a few months ago, and you and yo' mama said y'all was gon' be fixin' that fence and I ain't seen no proper fixin'. All y'all did was hung that barb wire over the post. And you think that's all you had to do?"

"I fixed the fence, sir."

"Naw y'all didn't."

I try to plead with this fool again. "I den seen wild boars all in these woods. I got no reason to lie to ya."

The man hawks and spits onto the ground. "Look, I don't care if God hisself came down here and plucked a hole in that fence for every creature on that goddamn Arc to come over here. The next time I see any of *your* animals on *my* property," he says, then angles his head toward the shotgun leaning against the fence, "I'ma get that Chester and blow they heads off. You understand me?"

3

TEDDY MCMILLAN

I feel a knot in my stomach and heat rising from the bottom of my feet to the top of my earlobes. I avert my eyes from his stabbing glare, then clench my fist and take a deep sigh. I do exactly what my mama has always told me: 'When white folk get mad, just go on about yo' business. They don't know no better.' Of all the thoughts swirling in my head, I'm glad my mama's voice comes through.

I turn my head and make my face muscles retract. "What? You gotta problem with it?" he barks.

Pressing my lips together tightly, I say, "No, sir. I ain't got no problem, sir."

"Now, you c'mon here and get that cow and tell ya mama what I said."

I grab the twisted steel wires between the two sharp points with my palm, push it away from my body and step over one leg at a time. The man follows me. I rotate my head and see him trudging on the side of me carrying the long shotgun and pushing the tip of the barrel into the ground as if it's a walking stick. The humidity is dense. Sweat beads form on my forehead, but I'm too afraid to swipe them off. The pasture is curvy and covered in lush, green blades that extend far ahead of me. This looks nothing like the barren ten acres me and my mama own.

We come to a drop in the pasture, and there is a steep decline at the bottom with a thin brook streaming in a zig-zag pattern. Some cattle drink from the stream while others graze freely. Suzy is scrawnier than the Jerseymaids. They have fattened bellies that protrude equally on both sides. Suzy zips from one Jerseymaid to the next, poking fun like she's in a playpen.

"Suzy," I yell. She turns in my direction, then ignores me and darts quickly to the salt block station and gets her a good licking.

I bolt in her direction.

"See what I'm talking about?" The old man grumbles. He then starts a limping trot to the rustic shed not far from the salt block station. I shoo Suzy away from the block and she scampers, moving her legs quickly below her to keep her balance. By this time, the old man exits the shed pulling a long two-by-four over his shoulder while the opposite edge scrapes against the ground.

"Get outta here," he grunts and runs at Suzy. He reaches back and takes a wide looping swing at Suzy, and the edge of the board catches her across the base of her back. Suzy thrusts forward to escape. My heart jumps. I swing my head in the direction of the old man and side-step in between him and Suzy. He's huffing, still dragging the long piece of wood in his hand.

"You betta not hit her again," I yell.

"You get off of my property," he commands.

I take a deep sigh, and with both arms stretched on my side, I clench both fists. My chest pumps in and out, and I stare with fierce intent. *Nothing but the devil.* I turn away from the old man and escort Suzy through the pasture and off the property, mumbling to myself, "damn fool".

***

The tall trees block the sun and cast thick shadows onto the surface of the woods. The woodlands aren't that scary during the day, but when the sun drops, the same chirping cricket sounds and hooting owls send chills throughout my body. During the summer it gets hot. Well, I mean, really hot, like scorching hot. The kind of hot that makes it feel like you are trapped in a wood burning stove. But I love being in the woods. I feel free here. It's just me and nature, nothing else. I hear the snapping of dry debris on the surface of the woods as Suzy plods along. "You cain't be going on that man's land no more, Suzy." Suzy pays me no mind. I tap her with a stick to keep her on the narrow path back to the house. *Ain't no way she broke that fence again. No...no...no.*

It's only about three hundred of us in the town, and most of us are black in the area where I live. It's called Sumerville and it's in the southern part of Alabama not far from Monroeville. The town got its name from the time when Indians lived here, and they got into a fierce battle with confederate soldiers one long summer. My Uncle Charlie tells me I shouldn't call them Indians because Christopher Columbus was stupid enough to think he was in India. Uncle Charlie says, "Okay. If you went to Beatrice and thought you was in Repton, would you call the people Reptons?"

My uncle is known to joke around, so I say, "Naw. It don't make no sense."

"See. That's why you don't be call 'em Indians," he tells me with his signature grin spread wide across his face.

It's just me and my mama, and with the Big War that was started a few years ago, most white folks been acting strange, thinking they can tell us what to do right down telling us not to look them in the eye. My mama is different than most blacks. She don't go for that. She taught me to hold my chin high when I talk to anybody, even the pastor at the church.

Light glitters through the tall trees, and I see our house through the gap. We live in a small sharecropper shack made of wood planks with a wood chimney that projects at an angle away from the house in case of fire. I see my mama from a distance. She reaches into a basket to get a sheet, wrings it out, then pins it to the clothesline. She steadies her head when she sees me, but continues pinning.

"Where he go this time?" she says, while holding the sheet to the line with one hand with the other on her hip.

"Right back over on that white man property."

Mama grunts and shakes her head, then pulls another sheet from the basket and jerks it in a downward motion. "What I been telling you?"

I exhale and mumble under my breath. "Fix the fence right, or get rid of the cow."

"Huh?"

I say it louder, "Fix the fence right, or get rid of the cow."

"That's right. That's exactly what I told you. Did you do it?"

"No ma'am. I didn't do it."

"Why not?" I feel a blood rush in my chest. I rub the back of my neck, then swallow.

"That cow ain't did that. She ain't gon' break through no fence. So, all I did was hammered the post real good and that was it. Made sure the line was tight. That's all a cow need. A little barrier. They ain't knocking over nothing to get through. It musta been them wild boars."

My mama reaches back into the basket and grabs a towel. I can tell her movements are fueled with anger. "Look. I ain't got time to tend to no cow. She ain't even producing much milk around here. Now we gotta spend time fixin' fences to keep her inside? Don't seem like time well spent to me."

"I'ma fix it mama. But I still think she ain't got nothing to do with it. Ain't nothing but them boars."

"Well, you get to cuttin' some of that wood by the barn and fix that fence. While you at it, we might as well take care of the barn too. You hear me?"

"Yes, ma'am."

"Now, you put that cow in the barn and lock her up. When you done, get ready for supper."

"Yes, ma'am."

"We'll get to it first thing in the morning."

I turn in the direction of the barn.

"Sol," she calls out.

"What that white man say?"

"Ma'am?"

"What he say about the cow being on his land? Last time, he got real nasty and acted all uncivilized."

I drop my head instinctively, and when I look back up, she's staring at me. "Um. He didn't say much."

"Oh, he didn't?" Mama says, lifting one brow up to express her hint of disbelief.

"No. Just told me to make sure Suzy wasn't on his property again, that's it."

"Hmmm."

I peel my eyes away from her stare and continue toward the barn. I know she's still looking at me. I can't tell her the truth. Mama's got a shotgun too, and she ain't afraid to use it.

CHAPTER TWO

The thunderstorm from last night left a damp smell in the air. I step off the porch and take a deep breath, filling my lungs with the pleasant aroma mixed with burning firewood. The crickets whistle like they are singing in some musical ensemble, each one chirping away to get more attention than the next. Mama is already moseying around the barn area eyeing the good pieces of sideboards that I had already cut, but I hadn't had enough time to nail them to the barn to fill the gaping hole left by the boars. And with the harsh rains coming just about every day, there really ain't been a time to fix it. The storm let up for the most part and the sun is peeking through the gray clouds. It's time for us to work.

It's a small barn with aged wood on the sides and green algae twisting and locking through horizontal planks on the lower half of the structure. The roof consists of tin and sparse with reddish spots over most parts due to rust. The barn is only big enough for a few animals. Me and my mama got a horse named Thunder, five chickens, and one cow. Suzy stays outside, of course, and we've been talking about building a coop for the chickens, but for now, the horse and the chickens stay in the barn.

Everything was fine and dandy until wild boars started attacking our animals. They got one of our chickens that had strayed too far out into the pasture, and next thing we knew, they just came right on up to the barn a few weeks later and ripped through the dangling plank on the side and got two more. Feathers were scattered everywhere, and a wing was ripped clearly off one of the chickens and left several feet from the barn. It happened on a dark night, and about the time I woke Mama up when I heard the rumbling and she grabbed the shotgun, we heard their loud snorts fading away in the pitch black woodlands. Mama raised the shotgun and blasted a single shot into the abyss. The loud sound echoed and reverberated in my head for several seconds.

Her instructions to me were simple: "Boy, you betta fix that barn or they gon' eat up everything we got."

My mama's name is Katherine Marie Canning. Most people call her "Kat". She has caramel-colored skin with a splatter of brown freckles around her fluffy cheeks, and I guess you can say she's somewhat on the heavy side. One thing she never talks to me about is that gash over her left eye. Uncle Charlie brought it up one day, and she cut him off and sent him home. He ain't came by ever since. When I want to see him, I go to his house or to his other favorite spot: the Juke Joint.

Mama picks up two, long boards and the clattering of the boards hitting each other breaks the morning silence. She shifts her eyes to me as she moves with the boards tucked tightly between her arm and the side of her body.

"Guess you decided to get on up," she says, her voice laced with a hint of sarcasm. Her eyes go right back to the pieces of wood. "See the grits on the stove?"

"Yes, ma'am. Had a little breakfast. Now, I'm ready to go."

She drops the wood then rubs her chin with the inside of her hand and inspects the side of the barn. "Hmm. Looks like we gon' need more wood than we got here." She reaches and grabs a hammer from the cutting table and swings the claw of the hammer into edges of the barn's rotten wood, then yanks it toward her body. The brittle wood chips crumble and fall to the ground. "Look. All this gotta come off. All this is rotten."

I feel antsy. "I'ma cut more wood." I trot to the other side of the barn and get the sawhorse and long handsaw set up.

"Look here," Mama instructs, "this gotta be at least eight feet from this side post to the middle one. You gon' need to cut some mo' wood to put in some posts right here in the middle."

I nod my head in agreement. "Yes, ma'am."

Mama continues. "So, get that string and measure from the end to the middle, we gon' have to put a post right here. We can do that on both sides. If not..." she steps near the side of the barn and peels wood chips from the termite-ridden post. "This ain't gon' hold this roof up. This about gone."

I nod my head. "Okay, mama."

"You start on that while I start thinking about how we gon' support this wall."

I place the wood on the sawhorse and measure the marks. I'm not too fond of jagged edges. I learned to make sure the saw goes clear through the wood on the bottom side. If not, the rough edges can send splinters deep into your flesh if you get a nasty snag.

I bend at my knees, close one eye and place the teeth of the saw just above the chalk line. I yank the saw across the wood: *thwack-thwock...thwack-thwock...thwack* until there's a sharp drop in the sound to complete silence. The cut is clean.

Mama holds a board up with one hand and places it at the midpoint of the old posts. The length of the board extends a few inches beyond the height of the roof. She steps onto a ladder and uses a thick pencil to strike across the tip of the board.

"Okay. Do this one first." She lets the board fall to the ground, and I pick it up and start sawing away.

My forearms glisten from sweat that couldn't escape the sun's glare, and I feel the dampness of my back causing my shirt to stick to my flesh. Once we get the post supports in place, she starts hammering the sideboards. *I just can't tell her about that crazy white man.*

The late morning sun hides behind a cloud, and a dark shadow casts over the barn. I stop and rub the back of my neck. Mama continues working. She holds a board across the horizontal space. Her eyes move quickly from the board to the post like two buzzing bees, while she holds a nail with her index finger and thumb and moves it to the precise spot. She reaches back, and with two good whacks, the body of the nail disappears in the board.

"Here you go, mama." I raise my chin and let two more boards fall near her feet. I swipe my forehead with my sleeve and get back to sawing. She angles another piece of board and picks a nail from her mouth, then positions the nail and reaches back for another nice swing. The hammer hits her square on the thumb.

"Darn it!" she screams twisting her body and grimacing. "Ooh. Good God that hurts."

"Mama!" I scream, dropping the saw and running to her side. Blood slides down her thumb. She spits the nails out of her mouth.

"Christ." She presses her thumb against her tongue, trying to stop the bleeding. She then grips the wrist of her injured hand and it trembles while she holds it away from her body.

When I see the blood gushing out of her thumb, a rumbling bursts inside of my mind. I whip my head around and close my eyes, trying to force out memories that come rushing into my mind uninvited. It's too late. My heart thuds fast, and though I shut my eyes completely, I feel them dart under the lids.

"Sol...Sol," Mama yells.

I slowly open my eyes. I see Mama with her nostril flared, and she's staring at me.

"Hurry up, child. I need them planks to finish this here side." She gathers two boards and tugs them to the side of the barn. "We gotta keep these wild boars away, son. What in heavens do they want with four, little, frail chickens anyway? Ain't no meat on they bones. Seems like they would have enough sense to at least get up there to the Washington farm and have themselves a feast." My shoulders sink. "Still ain't got over it yet, son?" she asks.

"No, ma'am."

"Ain't nothing we can do about it now, Sol."

"Okay," I whisper.

"All you can do is shape up and get going," she says, smiling. "Ain't that what I been telling you all these years?" I press the sides of my mouth back.

"Now, hurry up now and go into the house and get some mo'

of them nails. Maybe getting you out this sun will do ya some good."

I rub my palms together and head into the house. It's dark, so I blink repeatedly, letting my pupils adjust. Rays of light peer through the cracks in the roof and the vertical creases in the drab window covering as they blow gently with the subtle, hot breeze. The light paints beautiful, triangular slices of light on the grungy floor. The familiar smell of burning wood from the stove feels good, and I drag in the aroma of last night's stove fire. I look around until my eyes rest on the mantel where the bags of nails sit. The floor squeaks beneath me. Just as I dip my hands inside of the bag to scoop a handful of nails into my palm, my eyes meet the eyes of the man in the picture sitting on the mantel. I pick it up. Mama tells me the man is my daddy.

He is smiling brightly like someone who has no cares in the world, sitting on the fender of a 1934 Ford Deluxe Roadster. He looks handsome and happy. His shoulders are thin, but muscular. His hair is cropped short, silky, and jet black, and his mustache is tidy and trimmed. His teeth are the whitest that I have ever seen.

I turn and look over my shoulder, then return my eyes to the photo. I rub dust particles from the glass frame with my fingers. *Pa. When you coming back home? Why you leave to fight in a war you know nothing about?* I feel fluttering in my belly and tears fill my eyes.

"Sol," Mama's voice blasts from outside. "Come on now." Her glaring voice makes me jerk and disrupts my wandering thoughts. "What's taking you so long? We gotta get these boards on before the rain comes." My gaze fades, and I return the picture to the mantel.

"Yes ma'am," I shout back. "I'm coming now." I look through the window and see Mama struggling to get a good grasp of the hammer. I hear her wince and let the hammer drop to the ground. I gather a bunch of nails and move quickly through the doorway. Mama's eyebrows rise when she sees me approaching.

"I think all we need is two more boards, and we all done here, son." Her cheeks flare and a smile appears soon after. She stands and glances over the length of the barn and nods slowly. "Them wild boars ain't gon' be coming up in our barn after this. They then ate enough of our chickens and they ain't eating no mo'." She nails another board to the side of the barn. "I'ma keep that shotgun loaded just in case," she adds.

I grab the last two boards. "Here's those two." I pass the boards to her then place several nails in the palm of her hand.

She collects the nails and places a few between her lips. I help her hold the boards steady. She gives me a nod and passes me the hammer. "You do the last one."

My eyes bulge. "The last one?"

"You can do it." She hands me two nails.

I position one of the nails with my index finger and thumb, inching into the middle of the board.

"Tilt your head to the side a little bit. It's a better angle on the nail." I reach back and swing the hammer. It connects solid on the head of the nail. "There you go. Now hit it a coupla' more times, and that's all you need." I smack the nail two more good times and the head connects flat into the wood. Mama claps. "Looks like a good job to me."

I raise my head and smile. There's a warm feeling in my chest. "Thank you, mama."

"Yeah. You did the harder part of the work." She dusts off her palms and stretches her back. "All we have to do now is get some more wire from Furly's tomorrow and fix that fence so that cow ain't going over there on that man's land."

"Yes ma'am. We going to town tomorrow?"

"I reckon we need to. That's the only way we gon' fix that fence the right way."

"Okay."

"Tidy up things in the barn and come on in to clean up for supper. I guess you hungrier than a fat man on Thanksgiving," she snickers before heading to the house.

"Yes ma'am. I'ma clean everything up."

I feel a lightness in my limbs. Going to town has always been exciting for me. It's rare that I see my mama smile. I don't want to wipe it away telling her the truth about what the white man did.

CHAPTER THREE

Solitude is a vocabulary word that I learned in the 4th grade. Miss Shelby was ecstatic when I was able to spell it and use it in real sentences. Now that I'm thirteen, I'm starting to realize how much this word means to me.

My room is small. It's big enough to contain my mattress, which sits on twelve-inch wooden boxes on the corners and several in the middle. The only other items are a desk and a single chair. The floor has a light layer of sand over thick, wide planks that sends off this *creaking* sound every time I walk over them. Besides walking in the woods, my room gives me solitude. It's the one place that I love to retreat to when I need to think.

I pick up a book from the few scattered on the desk and place it under the wavering, yellow light of a small candle. *Native Son* by Richard Wright is in bold black letters. It's a gift from Miss Shelby. I flip the pages quickly to find where I left off, then gently move the dry leaf used to mark the point. My eyes trail my finger as I move from line to line thinking about how it must've felt to live in a big city like Chicago in the 1930s. I imagine riding in a big, black car beside my dad, and he's smiling, just like he is in the picture.

"Sol. It's supper time," Mama's voice rings out.

"Okay. Be there inna minute, ma."

I stand the books up on my desk in a vertical position and blow out the candle, then go to the kitchen. As soon as I pull one of the chairs back, lower my butt into it, and ease up to the kitchen table, I feel a rumble in my stomach.

"You must be hungry," Mama notes. She scoops butter beans from the large, cast iron pot. Steam emanates from the beans and dissipates in thin air. She places two scoops on my plate and one on hers, then cuts two pieces of cornbread and place them on a plate in the center of the table.

After I say grace, I dip the spoon into the bowl and pull a heap of beans into my mouth.

"No meat in this one," Mama says, pressing one side of her mouth back. "The price of salt pork then went up like crazy. I can't even see giving them people all that money for a piece of a hog." I feel a lump in my throat, and I swallow. I want to say something to my mama, but I don't interrupt her. She continues. "Them boars then took so many of our chickens I cain't even take the eggs up the road and trade 'em for some of the stuff we need." She shifts her gaze to the window, and she lets off a subtle sigh. "Have I told you your daddy is such a good shot?" she asks.

18

I pause, holding the spoon just short of my mouth. "Uh hmm."

"Oh, yes he is. He could shoot a itty-bitty quail dead with a single shot. Say...they had this contest about who could shoot the most quails and your dad always won," she shares. My eyes wander. "But he hardly ever used his gun when I was around." Mama smiles as she speaks. "I reckon God has a way of matching people together. Yo' daddy is such a kind soul. A respected man; people don't bother him." She presses her lips back and taps on the table. "I think they have a fancy word for it...providence." Her eyes meet mine. "You haven't heard that big word before, have you?" she asks, determined to draw me out of my silent thoughts.

"Providence. I reckon it's just a word about God and his plan..."

"Yes...yes, that's it," she affirms, fluffing her cheeks up. "Yes." She smiles again and her eyes glow. "Don't worry, son," she says and looks away. "That war gon' be over soon. Your daddy will return home and read to you, and all three of us will work together 'round the farm." She smiles brightly and swallows a lump of food in her throat. She drinks from the cup of milk before her. "Wouldn't you like that?" I nod my head slowly and take a bite of the cornbread.

When supper is over, I stand and start to clean the plates when the sky crackles loudly and thunder roars, shaking the house. I grab the edge of the dinner table and look at Mama, whose eyes are glossy and tense. My chin quivers.

Mama stands and stares through the window. "This storm is brewin'." She slams the window shut. "Fasten the locks on the door!" she commands me, and I spring into action. More thunderclaps sound over the house, and the rain slams down in torrents. There's a loud sizzle of lightning and a flash of light enters the house through a seam in the roof. Only a few seconds later, drops of water trickle into the house through the narrow slit.

This agitates me. "There's another leak in the roof!" I sprint the length of the room and pick up a pan just beside the door and place it under the leaking area of the roof.

Thud, thud, thud. The pan makes sounds as the drops of water land inside it. A loud wind rushes past the house, and I turn to Mama.

"The barn?" she says.

"I locked it," I assure her.

Mama nods. "Thank God we finished putting them side boards up today."

"Providence," I say slowly.

Mama chuckles. "Yes indeedie. Yes Lord." The storm continues to rage outside of the house.

CHAPTER FOUR

I hear Mama moving through the living room just before daybreak. "Come on, boy!" she says with a snappy tone. "We gotta get up that road before sunup and get to town as early as we can."

It's a humid morning following the stormy night. The buckets and pans still lay on the floor with water grazing the rim of two large pans. *Drip, drip, drip...* The drops gush into the pans, causing some of the water to splash onto the floor. I'm thinking about removing the pans and pouring out the water, but my mother's voice distracts me from making such an abrupt decision. All she wants to do is make it to town and make it back so that we can fix the fence.

"Hitch Thunder up to the wagon, and let's get up yonder," she says while she wraps a shawl tightly over her shoulders and pushes her fingers into white gloves. "Leave them buckets just where they

21

at and let's go." She rubs both gloved hands together and breathes air from her mouth into her cupped hands.

"I gotta get these two here, mama. They full."

She stares at the floor. "Okay. Go on then." She shoots a quick glance at the pans. "Might as well, but you gotta hurry up son. We gotta get outta here." I dart to one of the pans, lift it, and pour the water out of the back door. When I return, I scan the ceiling and place the buckets in the exact spot to catch more water if the storm comes back.

I jump off the porch, sprint to the barn, and rub both hands just before opening the door. I look around and see that the barn is still in good condition despite the storm of the previous night, calmness settles in my chest.

"Thank heavens!" I mutter and approach the horse's stall in quick steps. The last time a storm had raged, the barn was turned inside out, and the haystacks were all scattered. It took a better part of the morning to put everything back into its place. The worst thing was Thunder coming down with the sickness the very next day.

I lead the horse outside and hitch her to the wooden wagon with deft movements of my hands. "There you go. All ready to go, Thunder." I climb into the wagon.

"Ma!" I call out. I pull my jacket tighter around my body and tighten the brown cloth around my neck.

"Mama!" I call again. "The sun gon' be up soon!"

"Hush up, boy. I'm on my way."

Mama hurries out of the house and pulls the door after her. She tugs the shawl around her body and climbs into the wagon, sitting right beside me.

"The nerve of you. All that talk about the sun coming up, and I been up before the rooster even been crowing." I smile while Mama continues. "Cain't take no ride that long without no food. Got us a few biscuits."

I yank on the reins. "Scat now. C'mon girl." The wagon moves into the path that leads into town. Thunder's steps are slow. "Thunder gettin' old on us," Mama says.

"He got cold bones just like us getting up so early in the morning."

"Whateva," she snaps back.

After the long drive, we make it to town and head straight to Furly's General Store, a popular place in town which has everything from snacks to farm tools.

As I maneuver the wagon into a space between another wagon and a car, Mama turns to me and frowns. She shakes her head slowly and points to the sign written on a post close to the space: Whites Only. "Now, you know you cain't be in these folk's spaces," she whispers, then points. "Carry on 'round the side and hook up there."

"Yes, ma'am," I comply, and pull the wagon to the side of the building. "Colored" is scribbled in black paint on a wooden board.

Mama steps off the wagon. "Come on now."

I speed up to catch up with her. Before she enters the back door, she turns to me. "Look now, don't be actin' like you ain't use to nuthin' when you go up in here. Don't be puttin' yo' hands on nuthin'. Hear me?"

I nod in agreement. "Yes, ma'am."

Big John Furly, the white owner of the general store smiles broadly when he sees us. "Mornin' Miss Kat," he mumbles through his tight lips.

"Morning, sir." Mama walks directly to the jarred preserves.

"Are these here from the Jones farm up there in Atmo'?

"Surely is. Those there are fresh. They pick peaches right there on the farm. They got some of the best peaches 'round here. Daddy Jones been in business—I'll say, 'bout twenty or thirty years now. Always sweet and fresh, just like the customers like 'em."

I wander through the toy section. I pick up a baseball and toss it a few times into the air before sitting it carefully back onto the shelf. I open a *Workbasket Magazine* and flip through a few pages. I feel butterflies dancing in my belly. I know so many of the words in the magazine and can't wait to share this with Miss Shelby. Books are magical. They can place me in a world so far distance from the world I actually live in.

Time escapes me. Mama has a few items and stands at the counter with John, counting and pushing coins across the smooth surface into John's direction. I wander to the front of the store and I see two puppies in a cage next to Furly. I smile and walk toward the puppies, then kneel and stick a finger through the wired cage. "Hey buddies. Ain't y'all just the finest pups ever." The dogs wiggle their tails, move close to my finger, and start licking.

"Those there are Bluetick Coonhounds," Furly says from where he stands, watching with interest as I play with the pups.

At that same moment, Mama turns to the side and marches towards me. "Stop it right now." Her voice startles me and the puppies. I quickly stand and take two steps away from the cage. I look at my mother with wide eyes. "Boy, you know not to be meddlin' with folks stuff!" she tells me. I take two more steps back. Furly walks closer to the cage and squats next to it.

"Son, you lookin' to get you a fine hound like this?" he asks. He opens the cage and rubs the puppies' heads. John then glances at Mama. "Ain't nuthin wrong. He just touching these pups. He's okay, Kat."

I look up at Mama's face. Her body is stiff and her eyes beam. I clear my throat. "No, sir," I whisper. "I don't want one. But you got ya'self some fine hounds there, sir." I can't help but stare at the puppies as they rub their noses against Furly. Furly looks directly at me.

"You like them hounds, don't you?"

I nod quickly and smile more broadly. "Yessir," I say. "They look mighty good, sir."

Furly nods and looks at the dogs. "Ain't no coon out there can get away from these hounds here. They got something in they smell. Something in the way they made up. They can sense a coon from a mile away." He drops his head momentarily, then continues. "I tell you what," he says, "just for five dollars, you can get one of them pups. Maybe not these exact puppies 'cause these here are already accounted for. But I can get you a real full-blooded coonhound." Furly's smile widens. "I think I like you, son. And I know you'll treat him real nice," Furly says, staring at me like I have the power to make the final decision. "Five dollars." From my periphery, I sense that Mama is staring at me.

When I turn to her, she frowns. "Follow me. We gotta get some more nails and get that wire for the fence." She walks away and I follow close behind her, turning and still looking at the puppies in the cage. Mama gets a few other items and tugs on my shoulder often to ensure I'm close by. Once back outside, she drops the items into the wagon and turns to me. "Whatcha do that for?"

I raise my eyebrows. "Ma'am?"

"Why you touch them dogs? You know black folk been killed

for meddlin' with white folk and they property, ya know?" Her eyes blaze with fire. "You cain't go around here touching they stuff, ya hear me, child?"

"Yes, ma'am," I answer, then drop my shoulders.

Mama climbs into the wagon, and mutters with a menacing tone, "Let's leave." I jerk my shoulders around and climbed into the wagon.

The journey back home is quiet.

I unload the wagon and put Thunder into his stall after feeding him. When I enter the house, Mama is moving items around on the table with quick hand movements. She stops and glares at me. "Whatchu even need a dog for?" I feel heat behind my eyelids. "You shouldn't have bothered them dogs at all!" She adds, before I could respond. Mama storms off and leaves me standing beside the door.

"Sorry, mama," I tell her when she returns to the front room. "I wanted to see if you could buy me one of them puppies."

She stares and lets out a grating laugh. "Get one of them puppies?"

"Yes, ma'am."

Her eyes turn cold, she tilts her head to the side and purses her lips. "Getchu a puppy for five dollars? Have you gon' crazy?"

"No," I stutter.

"You have five dollars somewhere I don't know about?"

"No, ma'am." I shake my head slowly. "I just want to have a friend I can play with in the yard. Maybe do some hunting," I say softly.

"You want a friend that cost five dollars? Is that what you sayin'?" She folds her arms. "As many times that I had to tell you to tend to the animals we got...*Sol, fix the fence...Sol, fix the boards on the barn."*

"Mama, it's just a puppy."

She takes a deep sigh. I bite my lower lip and keep quiet.

She moves through the maze of buckets on the floor and enters the kitchen, still fuming. Mama keeps on telling me how ridiculous the idea of getting a dog for that much money is, and she starts to move things around in the kitchen. A clattering sound reverberates throughout the house. "Darn!" Mama shouts in annoyance from a pot dropping onto the kitchen floor. I walk around the front room and pick up the buckets one at a time then empty the rest of the water from the previous night's rain outside and stack the pots and pans neatly on a side wall.

I don't want to respond to her rage; the last time I did, she put the rawhide on my behind and beat me until I screamed, but she ain't done that in years. Mama sits on the single chair in the front room and starts to knit a blanket. She always does that when she's angry. Though she's quiet, her face is still flushed with anger.

I walk into the front room with my head dropped and eyes on my feet. I stand within a few feet of her for a few minutes. "When my daddy coming home?" I'm always hesitant to bring up the subject of my father, but I couldn't hold back anymore. Maybe he will get me a dog when he comes back. Sweat dampens my palms and my heart races. Her hands continue to work the needle and yarn. The room falls silent for the next couple of seconds as I wait for her response. When she doesn't answer, I frown. "I wanna see him." Still, Mama keeps her full attention on the knitting, and she doesn't even raise her head once. My lips shake and I swallow hard and lower my eyes before walking out of the house. Tears fill the corners of my eyes, but I'm determined not to cry. *I'm a man after all.*

I stomp hard across the floor and exit house, hit the barn, and fall limp into a stack of hay, exasperated. To clear my head, I pack hay together and tie them into large bundles. When I'm done with that, I go into the yard and use the axe to split wood into bits to use as starter wood for the stove. When the sun drops, I go back into the barn and ease onto the hay. The thin straws prickle my forearms and the side of my face. I dig my shoulders deeper in the hay to find just the right contour for comfort. Moments later, my stomach grumbles, but I'm determined not to go into the house until I'm calm enough to face my mother.

CHAPTER FIVE

I am awakened by the rooster's loud crowing. I jerk my head and see feeble light filtering through the gaps in the wooded barn door. Pieces of straw dangle from my hair, so I run my fingers through it and thrust downward to flick them out. Of all the times I have gotten mad and went to the barn for some quiet time, this is the first time Mama actually let me stay in the barn all night. It's a school day, and all I want is to go to school, see my friends, and probably spend some time at the creek. But I know I have to deal with her first.

I open the barn door and head to the house. The shimmering rays have just begun to pierce the darkness from the warm night. I see the flickering of muted orange light through the window coverings of the house. When I open the front door, Mama is

29

moving about in the kitchen.

"You have a good night sleep?" she says, while fumbling with items on the table and never letting her head quite shift in my direction.

"It was okay," I mumble.

"Huh?" she says, finally turning to me with raised eyebrows.

"It was okay."

She folds her arms and holds her chin high. "Oh...hmmm." She chuckles. Mama pulls her coat from the hook on the wall and pushes her arms into it, then pulls a hat firmly onto her head. I'm still standing just inside the door. "I made some biscuits. Make sure you get little Johnny one too."

"Yes, ma'am."

I hear the sound of tires cutting through rough gravel. A car horn blares. She finally lets her eyes settle on me without the tension. "Mable picking me up. I gotta work and won't be back until late. Feed them animals before you go and don't be hanging out in them woods either."

I nod. "Yes, ma'am."

"They tell me another black man was hanged the other night. Don't know where he from. But just stay out them woods. You hear me?"

"Yes, ma'am."

Mama whisks by me and goes through the door. I turn and stand in the doorway, watching her make her way to the car. She opens the car door and looks at me.

"Come right home after school. We gotta fix that fence."

"Okay," I yell back.

I brush my teeth, splash water onto my face, and dry it with a small cloth. My trousers are dirty, so I change them and put on another shirt.

I stuff two biscuits into my trouser pocket and go to the barn to feed the animals. The barn smells of tangy pee and manure that can only come from Suzy. Flies buzz around and land on top of the mountains of dung spread across the stall where Suzy is. I lead her out of the barn and hook her holster to a post outside in a shaded place. I make sure that the slipknot is tight so that she can't snap it off, then push down on her backside to force her into a sitting position, and she gives in.

"Now, you gon' stay here until I get back." It's best that she stays out here in the air and not be cooped up in the barn. It's dried corn for the chickens, and hay for Thunder. I sit and watch the chickens pluck the kernels and wiggle their necks like they are moving to the beat of the latest swing song. I rub the back of my neck then lean back against the wall of the barn imagining how things would be with a dog that could help me with the animals. There would no more of Suzy going through the fence. The dog could round her up and bring her back. I could even train him not to attack our chickens, so he could be like a shepherd for them, saving them from all the beasts that lurk in the woods. And he could warn me when the wild boars came back.

I can't get those puppies from Furly's out of my head. My eyes are heavy. My upper torso tilts to the side and my body begins to fall. I catch myself just before I fall completely to the ground. I hear Thunder's huffing breaths and the chickens *tuck...tuck...tuck. Shoot, I'm late to school.* I dart out of the barn and hit the road with the same burst of speed. The road is not as bad on my feet as the debris I step over on the shoulder of the road which can be pebbles, edges of large rocks, branches, or mounds of red ants. The soles of my shoes are in bad shape, and I can't take any chances.

I see a small plume of smoke ahead just over the tree branches drifting high into the air. The smell of burnt trash stings my nostrils. I swing my arms and legs faster to get to the house. I get to the opening of a red dirt side road that leads to Johnny's house. The house is white with yellow trim, has an enclosed front porch, and sits back several hundred feet from the main road. The smoke comes from a trash fire and Johnny's mother is dabbing at the fire with a metal pole.

"Hey, Sol. Mo'nin, son," she says, with one eye closed, crouching low and stabbing at the fire like a professional fencer.

"Good morning, Miss Belle."

She pokes the pole several times at the top of the metal barrel and moves her torso closer with each stab at the fire. Small sparks brighten and glow orange then disappear in thin air. The crackling sound intensifies every time she sticks the pole into the fire.

"You late today."

"Yeah. I got up late."

"Johnny in there. I thought his daddy was gon' have to take 'im. Go on inside, son."

Just as I turn and move to the porch, Johnny steps out with a bright smile and limps in my direction.

"Hey, Sol. What took you so long?" Johnny is shorter than I am and he's always smiling and moving his eyes behind his thick glasses.

"I'll tell you about it." I glance at Miss Belle. "Have a great day Miss Belle." She stops with the fire and lets the end of the pole graze the ground. "Y'all be careful now. You betta hurry up. Miss Shelby gon' get y'all tails for being late."

SOL & SIMONTON

"Bye, mama," Johnny says.

"Bye, baby."

We can't move too fast because Johnny can't walk fast. He has this issue with his leg, and Mama said it happened when he got polio as a kid. His shoes are hard and when he walks you can hear them *click-clocking* against the ground. I always pick him up on my way to school.

Johnny and I walk on the side of the road, deep in the shoulder so we don't get picked off by a passing car or truck. "You hear about this war?" he asks.

"Naw. I don't know much about it. All I know is that I hope it ends soon."

"Makes no sense to me. My daddy let me read the whole newspaper yesterday."

"For real?"

"Yep. I don't know why these white people fighting each other, and now they turn it into a world event. Getting the whole world involved 'cause they can't get along. Why cain't they just all meet up in Europe and fight each other like with swords?"

"Swords?" I laugh. "Nobody fight with swords no more. Everybody got guns, and cannons and airplanes..."

"But wouldn't it be cool though? Just like in the old days with big castles, kings, and knights." Johnny stops and whips his arm across his chest, "For my honor, my country, I lay my life down by the sword for there's no other way to live, but to live with honor."

I burst out in laughter. "What was that?" Johnny joins in on the laughter. "Did you get that from Shakespeare or something?"

"Shakespeare. What do you know about Shakespeare?" he asks.

33

"Nothing really. I heard he wrote plays—at least that's what Miss Shelby told us like a year ago, even before y'all moved out here."

Johnny's face grows blank and he continues to walk. "Actually, that was something I wrote."

"You wrote that?" I ask, stopping abruptly while Johnny continues to take two steps forward.

Johnny turns to me. His face is stiff. "Yeah. I wrote a lot of plays," he says, with a crackle in his voice. "I wanna be an actor. But my mama and daddy tell me I'll never become an actor because of my leg."

I sigh, then reach down into my pocket. "Aye, look what I got." I pull out the two biscuits.

Johnny's eyes brighten. "Aww. You got me one of your mother's biscuits?" I smile and hand him a biscuit wrapped in a small napkin. Johnny bites into the biscuit.

"Man, yo' mama know she can make some good biscuits."

"I know," I say, grinning and showing my teeth. "They the best." I chew slowly, and while still facing Johnny, I say, "Look, you gon' be an actor one day. If that's what you wanna do. Cain't nobody stop you if that's really what you want."

Johnny drops his head and I feel his anguish. "Let's get to school before Miss Shelby get real mad at us for being late."

"Naw. Look Johnny, do this." I close my eyes and take a long, deep breath, allowing the air to fill my lungs. When I open my eyes, Johnny's head is tilted to one side and I see creases on his forehead.

"Do what?" he asks.

"Close your eyes and do what I just did."

Johnny closes his eyes and inhales. His chest presses out, then he exhales. "See that?" Johnny nods his head.

"Now, look around," I tell him, and I turn my body a full three hundred and sixty degrees, with my arms stretched on my side and palms pointing to the sky. "This whole world is ours. God made it for everybody. Cain't nobody take it from you and say *you can do this*, but *you cain't do that*. Just like the breath you just took. Ain't nobody told you to do it, right?"

"Well, you *did* tell me to do it," he says, matter-of-factly.

We both laugh, and I take a playful jab at Johnny and he ducks. When the grinning stops, I look him in his eyes. "You gon' be an actor though, right?"

Johnny smiles and nods once in agreement. We extend our hands at the same time, slap each other five and end with a synchronous snap of the fingers.

CHAPTER SIX

The schoolhouse is a tan, rectangular building with a broad single window and it's connected to the side of our community church, Living Tree Baptist Church. Mama told me that black people started going to this church just after slavery ended and began mixing in with the whites. That didn't settle right with white folks, so they stopped going to the church and built another church, just for them, on Road 57, called Living Life Baptist Church, not far from our church.

I attend Sumerville Elementary School for Colored, and as the name suggests, only black kids can attend my school. It's really not a problem for me, because I only mingle with kids who look like me anyway. Miss Shelby is our teacher and she has a classroom of kids between the ages of seven and fourteen. Since me and Johnny are late, we don't want Miss Shelby to notice us, so we try to sneak in.

When we get to the backdoor, Johnny and I place our ears on the splintered, wooden door. It's cold and the vertical grooves feel funny against my face. I hear my classmates chattering and moving about. This is a good time for me and Johnny to enter, because Miss Shelby hasn't started the morning prayer yet. I turn the doorknob and push it ever so slowly. It squeaks, but I continue to widen the crack.

Movery is at her desk. She must sense that me and Johnny have arrived late again, and she turns and sees me bending with my head poking inside of the room. Movery is a petite, brown-skinned girl with big, hazel eyes and long curls that fall on each side of her face. Me, Movery, and Johnny are the best of friends. First, it was just me and Movery, then when Johnny moved to our town a few years ago and we've all been friends ever since.

Movery's smirks, then opens her mouth and covers it quickly with the palm of her hand. She whips her hand in a circular motion toward her body, signaling for us to make our move now. I tiptoe into the classroom with my eyes focused on my desk, but in my periphery, I see Miss Shelby seated at her desk with her head down marking papers. Johnny follows. When I ease into my seat behind Movery, I glance over Movery's shoulder and see Miss Shelby with both elbows planted on her desk. She's staring directly at me with her hands cupped, one overlapping the other.

"I'm glad Solomon and Johnny were able to join us today, class," she says in a patronizing tone. There are snickers throughout the classroom. "You wanna tell me why you boys are late today?"

Johnny glances at me, and I shrug my shoulders. "Well, I tell you..." Johnny begins.

I cut him off. "It was a big truck," I assert. "Full of onions...and the man hit a ditch...and they scattered all over the place..."

Johnny picks up from there. "Yeah. It was bad. So, me and Sol helped the man get the onions back on the truck..."

Miss Shelby rises from her chair and walks through the rows of desks. She's a thin woman with wide hips and when she walks, her hips sway from side to side like a life buoy floating on a river. She stops midway, folds her arms, then raises a pointing finger, allowing the tip of her index finger to settle on her temple. "So, tell me this. Was it a big truck?"

"Yes, ma'am," we say in unison.

"Maybe like a...service truck...maybe a truck used for farming?" Johnny says.

"Yes. It was both," I interject.

Several students can't contain their laughter, they burst out, and it echoes throughout the classroom. Miss Shelby extends her arms and flaps her hands downward. "No. Class, please...let's stay under control," she says, allowing her eyes to scan every set of eyes in the classroom. When the class settles, she says, "So, what color was the truck?"

Johnny and I answer at the exact same moment. The only problem is, I say "black" and Johnny says "brown". There is another round of snickers mixed with a few "*oohs*". Miss Shelby's jaws are tight. "Okay. You gettin' one for being late and another one for lying to me. I'ma see both of y'all after school."

***

The room is airy and has fallen to complete silence. The only noise I hear comes from outside as our classmates jostle around the window trying to get a good view. It's just me and Johnny and we are at our desks like old tree trunks, while Miss Shelby fiddles around in her desk. She pulls out both paddles and grips one in each hand, then stands and oscillates the paddles, going down and up for a few seconds as if she's comparing their mass. She gently lays the smaller paddle on the desk. The rumbling outside gets louder. Miss Shelby turns in the direction of the window. Through the window, I see the kids scatter. Miss Shelby is fuming. She stomps to the window, her steps are loud and her ponytail bounces as she moves by me. She jerks on the crank vigorously, and it squeaks, the window opens out.

"Look. Any one of y'all wanna to bring your little, black tails back up here and get one, just come on back to this window again. Just c'mon back up here if you want to and see whatcha gon' get." She winds the crank fast and the window slams shuts against the inner frame. She pulls the covering over the window and the muted amber light makes the room feel even more chilling.

My heart drops. I jerk my head back to the forward position, interlock my fingers and sit them in front of me on the desk just like they showed us to do in kindergarten.

"C'mon here, Johnny," she says.

Johnny swallows, then whips his leg from under the desk. He takes measured steps to the front of the classroom. I hear the *clickety-clack* of his shoes hitting the wooden floor and his shoulders rock from side to side. Johnny places his palms on the edge of the desk and bends over.

Miss Shelby stands behind Johnny. "Pull up your britches." Johnny tries, but his pants fall right back to the same position. She grabs the back of his pants and yanks them up, and raises the paddle in the air. "What we say about being late?"

Johnny's eyes are completely closed, and his face contorts to the most ridiculous looking frown. "Never be late to class," he grunts.

Miss Shelby's arm swings down and the paddle connects solid on Johnny's butt with a hallowed *pow*. The impact makes me twitch. Johnny puffs in and out and rubs his butt.

"You got one mo'," she says. "Now, I den gave you and Sol a warning before about being late. If you late again, you gon' get two of 'em."

I can't bear to see Johnny punished. "He was late because of me," I yell.

Miss Shelby looks at me. "Ain't no excuse. He a young man. He gotta take care of his own responsibilities. That don't change the fact that he late, right?"

I sit back in my chair. "No ma'am."

"Don't worry, you gon' get yours too." She twirls the paddle around in her hand. "C'mon Johnny. You got one more." Johnny gets into position. "And don't be wincing this time. Y'all 'round here lying and carryin' on. Getcho butt back up there."

"Yes, ma'am," Johnny says.

Miss Shelby pulls back and strikes Johnny again. "Ouch!" he yells. Johnny rubs his butt and moves away from Miss Shelby.

"Wait a minute. Don't go nowhere. You got one more."

"One more?" he says, just as perplexed as I am.

"Now, which one of y'all started that lie?"

"Whatchu mean?" I ask.

"I wanna know which one of y'all came up with that story."

I drop my head for a moment, then pick up my chin. "I did. I started the whole thing. Johnny didn't do nothing. I'm the reason he late, and I'm the one that started the lie. So, you can give me all the swats you want."

"All right then. Now bring yo butt up here."

I place my hands on the edge of the desk. I feel Miss Shelby grab my belt on the back of my pants. She yanks up. I bite down on my lip, and she gives my three nice ones, and I grunt after each one. *Dayum, that hurts.* I walk back to my desk.

"You want some mo'?"

"No, ma'am."

"Now, y'all get on outta here, and I betta not hear another lie come out your mouth, and you betta not be late again. You hear me?"

"Yes, ma'am."

We get our books and move quickly through the door.

CHAPTER SEVEN

Johnny and I make it out of the door and sprint toward the woods. It's late afternoon and clouds are thickening and covering most of the sky. Movery is probably waiting for me and Johnny at the edge of the grass patch behind the church just like she does every day after school.

Just beyond the patch of grass is a well-trodden, narrow footpath that leads to a flowing stream that pours into a creek. It separates one half of Sumerville from the other half. On the other side of the creek is Movery's house, and it takes us less than thirty minutes to get there taking this route. If we use main roads, it takes us at least twice the amount of time. Grownups have told us not to take this path because we have to go by the Old Oak Tree. We've all heard about the horrific stories of corpses of lifeless black men dangling from ropes tied to the high branches.

We see Movery from a distance, sitting on an old log with her head tilted down reading a book.

"Movery," Johnny yells. She raises her head and pushes the book into her bag; I see her wide grin. Johnny and I rush to her.

"What den gotten into y'all?" she scolds us. "Y'all coming to class late and telling Miss Shelby all kinds of lies. Y'all should be ashamed of ya selves, stressing that woman out over your nonsense. Making her paddle y'all."

"It didn't even hurt though," Johnny says.

"That's a lie." She folds her arms and wiggles her neck. "Boy, you know you tellin' a tale. I heard you grunting and yelling like lil ole baby."

Johnny's eyes wander. "No, I wasn't. I didn't even say nothing, right Sol?" They both look at me.

I crack a smile. "Now, you know she swung that thang hard today, Johnny. You gotta give it to her. Yessiree, Miss Shelby wasn't playin' at all."

"Yeah, it did kinda hurt," Johnny admits.

Movery points a finger at me, then Johnny. "Y'all know ya mamas gon' hear about this, right?"

"Yeah. Cain't keep much from our mamas," I add.

We continue through the woods. When we get to an open space, I turn to Johnny and Movery. "Aye, let's run to the creek."

"Run?" Movery replies, with a sour expression on her face. "You know me and Johnny cain't beat you running."

"Naw, I'm not talkin' about runnin' run like that. We can get to the creek around the same time. We can let Johnny go first."

Johnny delivers a nervous frown. "Naw, I dunno."

"He's right," Movery says, making strong eye contact with me. "Maybe we shouldn't..." Before Movery can finish, Johnny pivots and sprints into the woods. His arms move swiftly and his body jerks like a mechanical robot. He plants his foot and makes a sharp move into the woods.

I turn to Movery. "Okay. I'ma give you ten seconds."

Movery shoots out in the same direction as Johnny. I see the bottoms of her shoes and her elbows moving back and forth.

"Ten, nine, eight, seven, six, five," I yell. "You only got five seconds left. Four, three, two, one..." I trot into the woods. I see Movery from a distance, and she's moving quickly. She leaps over the stream and climbs a steep incline. I pick up my pace and cross the stream a few seconds after her. When I get to the top of the hill, Movery bends at the waist and breathes heavy.

"Y'all got me tired," she says.

I lower myself to a squat to catch a breath, and my joints crack.

"Where you think Johnny at?" I say. "You see 'im?"

Movery points back into the woods. "I saw him way back there. I thought he would be here by now. Did you pass 'im up?"

I twist my upper torso. "I ain't see 'im."

"Where you think he at?" she asks.

I feel churning in my stomach. "I dunno. Let's look for 'im. Maybe he went all the way to the creek."

Movery's eyes narrow, and she rubs the palm of her hand across her forehead. "Naw. We never do that. This is where we meet all the time."

We take slow, careful steps deeper into the woods. My eyes scan between the dull tree trunks and webs of tiny branches stretching across my path. I snatch the branches and pull them away from my body yelling, "Johnny." The echo returns to me seconds later.

"Johnny," Movery yells.

I point. "You go in that direction, and I'll go this way." We separate and continue yelling Johnny's name.

After a few moments, we reconnect. Movery lifts her hands and let them fall to her side.

"I don't know where he at. We should've just went together. You think something happened?" Her eyes are wide and her face fret with worry.

"He gotta be around here somewhere. Let's go back," I suggest.

"We would've seen him if he was back there."

"If we don't go back, then how we know if he ain't got bit by no rattler or fell in a big ole hole or somethin?"

Movery gives me a slow nod. "Okay."

We slide down the steep decline and step over the stream. We call out Johnny's name again, but there's no reply.

"I'm scared Sol," she says. Tears swell up in her eyes, and Movery eases next to me. I wrap my arm around her shoulder. Her fingers walk the back of my hand and interlock with my fingers. "It's gon' be okay. Let's keep looking." I take the lead while still holding her hand. The sound of chirping crickets is intense.

"Boo!"

I jerk to the side and raise a clenched fist, ready to deliver a crushing blow. Movery pulls my hand, and I let go. She falls to the ground.

Johnny lets off a boisterous laugh. He cups his hand over his mouth. "Ha. Y'all was scared. You shoulda seen y'all faces."

Movery charges Johnny and slaps him across his shoulder.

45

"What's wrong witchu boy? You den went crazy? Scaring somebody like you ain't got no sense." Johnny attempts to pull away to escape the battering.

I shake my head and extend my palm. "C'mon Johnny. You know you shouldn't be doing nothing like that."

Johnny pleads, "Man, why y'all acting all scared. I didn't even try to scare y'all that much."

"Well, you did. And you better not say another word to me again, or I'ma pop you right upside yo' head," Movery says.

Movery nudges him one last time, and Johnny smirks. We climb the steep hill again, making Johnny take the lead so that he doesn't try more tricks on us. Johnny turns to us while still walking. "Seem like y'all was having a whole bunch of fun though. Holding hands like y'all lovebirds."

"What?" Movery snaps. "Ooh. You make me sick." She lunges forward with her hand, and I block her from hitting him again.

I chuckle. "Man, can you just shut your mouth and keep walking?"

When we get to the creek, Movery and I sit on one side and throw small pebbles at the heads of turtles while Johnny sits on the other side poking fun at Movery, sticking his tongue out at her, and making silly faces.

"I ain't gon' pay him no mind. I'ma just let him sit over there and act a fool. But next time he scare me you betta not stop me from giving him a good one right across his nose. I'ma bloody his face all up. Watch me."

"Now, you know he don't mean no harm, right?"

"Solomon Canning. You know you ain't suppose to be on his side when he doing all this foolishness. Look at 'im." Johnny has his thumbs in his ears allowing his fingers to fan and his tongue pointed straight at Movery. I can't hold back from laughing. Movery holds on for a split second, then gives way to laughing too. "He 'bout crazy as a bessie bug."

"I know, but he ain't tryna hurt nobody."

Movery picks up a rock and throws it into the creek. She stands and looks in Johnny's direction. "Aye, Johnny," she yells. She returns his silly gestures with her own version of poking fun. She then picks up a rock and hurls it at Johnny. It startles Johnny. He swings his head to the exact spot where the rock fell.

"Aye. You tryna hit me?"

"Tryna hit you on your big ole head," she yells.

Johnny returns fire, launching several rocks that nearly hit me, but I refuse to join the fight. I poke a stick into the creek and watch my two best friends horse around like they have been doing for two years.

"You not gon' join us?" Movery asks.

"No. I'm okay."

I want to do something different. I want a hound dog so I can run through these woods and catch coons. When we make it to Movery's house, she and Johnny are still talking about the rock fight.

"You okay?" Movery asks.

"I'm fine." Movery peels away from us.

"See y'all tomorrow," she says, while waving. "And y'all betta not be late to school."

I want to see my uncle Charlie. He's the only one who can convince my mother to get me a dog. Johnny and I make it to the other side of Sumerville, and I drop him off at home.

"See you tomorrow, Sol."

"Okay, Johnny...tomorrow." Johnny and I slap hands, grip, and pop our fingers. I'm going to see Charlie so that I can get a dog.

CHAPTER EIGHT

After I cross the creek I move swiftly through the thick brush for several miles and push through the twigs snagging at my arms. The sound of chattering squirrels is intense. Two black buzzards soar above, and I think about what helpless animal is lying dead on the floor of the woods. Soon after, I find the dirt road leading to the juke joint. I dip into the shoulder of the road and ease into the edge of the woods so that no one can see me. I finally come upon the small sharecropper shack. I hope Uncle Charlie is here so I can ask him about the puppies.

Jazz music oozes out of the old shack and it gets louder as I tiptoe to the house with my back slightly arched. When I get closer, I crouch and peek through a crack in the wood planks used as a wall and see a medium-built woman swinging her body hard with reckless abandon to the rhythm of an upbeat song. Her hips jiggle, her red dress sparkles, and she keeps a sensuous smile on her face throughout, mixing her body movement with subtle winks at the men on the edge of their seats. She stands in the center of a dark stage with two women behind her, who smile and sing along.

Her voice is both rich and shrilling. A hefty man holds a big sax and makes it scream. That sends the men and women in the house cheering and raising their caps and hats above their heads.

A woman carries drinks and plates around the small room on a tray, my eyes follow the plates, and my nose wrinkles on its own volition. I feel my stomach grumble, and it's only then that I remember I had not eaten since lunch at school. The excitement of speaking with Uncle Charlie about the dog made me forget all about my appetite.

Just as I rub my hand against my stomach, I hear the unmistakable click of a gun just behind my right ear. My body freezes, and I feel my ears blaring with a pump of blood and adrenaline. But if there is anything I learned from Charlie; it is to never to make a sudden move around a person holding a gun.

I push my hands up slowly and my knees drop to the ground as I lose support.

"Don't move, boy!" a deep voice utters. My heart pounds.

"Okay, sir," I reply with a quiet hope that it is someone who knows Charlie.

"Turn around slow, son," the voice commands, "slow, son... slow."

I turn my body with my hands still raised, and I stare into the brown eyes of a dark-skinned, husky man with eyeballs as small as pea seeds. The sun is behind the big man, and I can't make out the face. I lower my eyes as the man's hard face softens upon recognizing me.

"Whatchu doing snoozing back here? I'm 'bout two seconds away from blowing ya damn head off." The large muscular man huffs, and slowly lowers his revolver. "Cain't be poking ya head in bit'ness that ain't got nuthin' to do witchu."

The man turns, and I recognize his face. Everyone calls him Bo. He is rumored to have been a good musician who travelled around Alabama, performing in bars and concerts, but his temper wouldn't let him have a successful career. Some say he had sold all his family's land and used the money to build the juke joint back here in Sumerville where he grew up.

"You Cha'lie nephew, ain't cha?" Bo says, in a way that makes each word sound like a song lyric. "You'a black boy. You cain't be mettlin' around a place like this, especially if the Klan see you out there in them woods. You cain't be actin' like one of them white boys running 'round here. You gotta be careful son, hear me?"

I squint and try to keep my gaze away from the man's eyes. "Yessir."

"Stand up, son. Ol' Charlie family." Bo starts to walk away. He slides the gun into the small of his back and flips his shirt over the handle as cover. He turns his shoulders but keeps his pace. "You comin'?" he asks, when he sees I'm not following. Bo escorts me into the room, and the riotous merriment blares into my ears. I wince and scan through the unfamiliar faces of the men and women who are dancing, singing, or just sitting and having a quiet drink. The room is dimly lit, and I have a hard time picking out Charlie. I feel a hand on my shoulder, I look up and see Bo pointing at a corner of the room and my eyes follow his finger. Charlie is laughing and screaming into a man's face. Bo nods slowly, smiles, and walks toward the stage.

Charlie is solidly planted at a large table with several other men, playing poker with cards, chips, coins, and some crumpled bills scattered on top. Each man around the table has a cigar somewhere near his mouth, and they puff the smoke and exhale it until the air is filled with a white mist.

Charlie places a card on the table. "Top that," he says, in a low but firm voice. He rests his back against the chair and a smile plays at the corner of his mouth.

"Hey, nephew," Charlie says when he finally notices me standing beside him. "You gon' bring me some luck?" he asks. "Now, I reckon you find yo'self making it up that road til ya finally end up here, huh?" Charlie keeps both eyes on the table while speaking.

"No sir," I say. "Just came up here to ask you what I been asking you, unc." Charlie turns his head slightly toward me. "Just tryna see if you den made contact with the man about the new litter of fine hounds he finsta have."

Charlie raises his back from the chair as one of the players holds up a single his card. He sighs and shakes his head. Another man, with two broken front teeth, lays his cards on the table. "Yes! There it is again! Y'all some broke niggas." He thrusts his fist into the air and takes a long drag from his cigar.

Charlie swears in a loud voice and throws his hands into the air. "You don't bring no luck, do ya?" he asks me and stands just as the man with the two broken teeth rakes the money off the table, whistling to the tune of the song playing.

"Now, y'all get ya broke butts on up that goddamn road and go ta work tomorrow so you can pay me again next week," the man yells, as the other men grunt and walk off.

I hurry after Charlie as he wriggles through the stuffed room, moving people out of the way with his walking stick.

"Where's ya mother?" Charlie asks when we get outside. "I bet five dead geese in a pea patch she don't know you up here, huh?"

"Nosir," I answer with sincerity. "She went down to the Washington's and probably won't be back til late."

Charlie glances at me with a knowing smile. "Listen, I'ma check on them hounds tomorrow, okay?" Charlie says, then moves the last of the cigar from his mouth. "But don' you go telling ya mama about this, ya hear me?"

"Yessir."

The backdoor of the shack opens. The blend of loud music and raucousness blare out. The singing woman lets her back rub against the interior of the door frame. Her eyelids dip. "Cha'lie, you ain't leaving right now are ya, baby?" she asks. Charlie turns to the woman chuckling ever so slightly.

"Naw. I ain't going nowhere. Be back in there inna minute sweetheart. Just talkin' to ma nephew here."

Silence fills the air for a moment. "Don't be long." She lets her gaze simmer before closing the door.

"Go on now, nephew. Ain't smart at all to be walking these roads at night. If the damn Klan ain't get cha, something in them woods certainly will."

I'm attentive, watching every word that comes out of his mouth. "Thank you, Uncle Charlie. See you later."

"Lemme take you home," Charlie says.

"Naw, unc. I got it. 'Bout time you get that truck engine warm, I'a already be over the creek." Charlie chuckles.

I turn toward the dark road and dart into the woods. I twist back and see Charlie watching on. The Klan attacks against blacks is at its highest in Alabama this year, and rumors have gone rife in the town about some of their members seen in their masks, meeting under the cover of darkness in the woods every other night.

"Best you run faster than that, boy!" Charlie yells. I disappear into darkness.

CHAPTER NINE

The sky is dark and the stars sparkle like tiny grains of light on silky black fabric. When I get to the main road, I run at a quickening pace for the rest of the way to the house. There is no light coming through the window coverings, so Mama must still be at the Washington farm. I leap onto the porch and when I open the door, there is complete darkness. I fumble my hand over the table until I feel the smooth surface of a long candle. I smell the rosary fragrance from it, and I pull one of the matches out of the brass holder and strike it against the edge of the holder. The yellowish flame glows, and I angle it to the wick. The room is immediately filled with an orange gradient tone with soft shadows.

There is a handwritten note on the table next to the spindle of wire that Mama purchased at Furly's for me to fix the fence. My blood pressure surges, and I move slowly away from the table with my hands cupped over my eyes. "No!" I yell. I had forgotten about Suzy and the fence. *Mama gon' kill me.*

I pick up the note from the table and it reads: *Sol, I told you to come home right after school to fix that fence. Mama.*

"Oh no," I say to myself, before dashing out of the front door and zipping across the yard to the barn. I get to the area behind the barn and don't see Suzy. My legs wobble momentarily. I reach for the rope and see that it had been snapped from the post. "Suzy," I yell out. There is darkness all around me and deafening silence except for a few hoots from the owls and chirps from nagging crickets. *Suzy is gone.*

I run to the house, get my lantern, and use the candle to ignite its flame. I follow Suzy's trail through the yard and into the pasture with the lantern held close to the ground. I stop and bend at one knee and follow the visual path that leads straight into the woods toward the white man's farm. I follow the tracks to the entrance of the woods, and when I get several feet inside, I see harsh light bobbing from the headlights of a truck, and it is moving toward the house. I blow out the flame from the lantern, turn and run back in the direction of the house while holding the lantern low near the ground. Just as I get a few steps from the porch, the truck exits the main road, the lights dip and bobble, and the truck continues directly toward the house. I rush through the front door, scamper into my room and dive onto my bed holding the *Native Son* book.

I hear the truck door slam, and Mama thanking someone for bringing her home. I draw the curtain back from my window ever so gently. The truck engine roars, and it pulls away from the house. When I hear the door open, I snap back to lying on the bed with my feet kicked up on the edge.

"Sol," Mama yells.

"Ma'am?"

"C'mon on in here, son."

I untie my shoes quickly and place them under my bed.

"Did you hear me?"

"Yes, ma'am. I'm coming."

I walk into the living room with apprehension. Mama is staring at me like a hawk on its prey.

"What did I tell you to do?"

I turn my head and drop my chin. "I just…"

"I said, what did I tell you?"

"To come home after school and fix the fence."

"That's exactly what I told you. I didn't give you no mo' instructions but that. All I asked you to do is come home and fix the fence. I could've asked you to cut more wood, clean out the barn, mop these floors in this house—that you never do, but I didn't. I asked you to fix the fence so that cow don't get out no mo', and you didn't."

"I'm sorry, mama."

"Sayin' you sorry ain't gon' fixed nothing. That don't make things no better. You have to make up yo mind that you gon' do what I tell you to do and stop doing what *you* wanna do."

"I can fix it tomorrow, mama. I promise. I'll come home right after school and take care of it," I plead. Mama doesn't budge. She wraps her coat on the hook nailed to the wall.

"I have every right to get that rawhide and put it on your tail, but that ain't gon' do nothing. You 'bout to be a man. You hear me?"

"Yes, ma'am."

Mama moves across the living room to her bedroom and slams the door behind her. She gives it a second push from inside to make sure her point is well taken.

The next morning, I'm awakened by clattering pots in the kitchen. It's still dark outside. I get out of bed and pull my trousers over my legs, whip on my shirt, and pull the strings on my boots snug to make sure the knot is tight. *Dammit Suzy!* I hope she ain't went over on that white man's property again. When I get to the kitchen, Mama is boiling a pot of water.

"Morning, mama," I say.

"Morning, son."

"Mama, I wanted to tell you that I'm sorry for not coming home right after school yesterday. I mean, I don't have nothing to say. I was just with Johnny and Movery, and I just lost track of time and I forgot. I didn't mean to."

"Well, you up mighty early today. Whatchu finsta do?"

"I'ma feed the animals and get ready for school. Figure I get up early today and start fresh. Start doing things like I'm suppose to."

"Well, I ain't got nothing else to say to ya about that. But don't for one minute think you gon' be around here like some of these other men. So many of 'em don't bit mo' think about nothing but hanging around here drinking and talking 'bout nonsense, and I be damned if I raise one of 'em. Ain't nothing worse than to see a young man that ain't ready for no kind of responsibility."

I nod my head. "I'ma do right, mama."

Mama's hands settle on her hips, and she takes a long gaze at me, and then continues moving plates around in the kitchen. "Getcho self some of these grits here before you go out."

"Yes, ma'am."

I lower myself into the wooden chair. The chair groans under my weight. Mama is holding a small, cast iron pot with a thick mitten and scoops a heaping of grits from the pot and drops it onto my plate. The steam floats into the air and dissolves quickly.

"Pastor gon' be here in a while to take me to work," she says. She lowers the pot onto the stove. "I guess there ain't no need to be telling you what I already been telling you."

"No, ma'am. I know what I gotta do."

Mama shakes her head, then motions to her room. "You have a good day."

"Yes, ma'am. You too, mama."

After lifting three huge scoops into my mouth and chowing down viciously with each scoop, I wash my plate and rush out the door.

Cock-A-Doodle-Doo. The rooster's crow let me know I'm up too darn early to be looking for a stupid cow. The gravel under my feet crunches with every step and silvery light spills on the edge of the horizon. I make it to the back of the barn to see if Suzy decided to come back, but she didn't. My heart drops like a ten-ton boulder from a tall building. There's nothing else for me to do but follow her trail again.

I pick up the trail where I left off last night, turning my shoulders frequently to push through the dense trees. This is nearly the exact path I followed two days ago to find Suzy the first time.

After several minutes, I come to a flat clearing and the ground is covered with dull greenish-brown colors from fallen leaves. I kneel to get a closer view of the trail. Rays of golden sunlight sift through the marquee of trees and spatters a soft luminance on the ground. I see the same broken fence in the distance.

TEDDY MCMILLAN

I start a light jog toward the fence, but before I can get there, I hear a light rustling over the dry vegetation and a raspy squawk that can only come from a buzzard. I swing my head in the direction of the sound. A buzzard flaps his long wings and elevates into the air. I slow my trot to a halt and take small careful steps to the spot where the buzzard took flight. As I draw closer, I can tell that the large hump on the ground has a shiny brown coat.

A sharp pain hits me right in the chest and my muscles go weak. *That's Suzy.* I clutch my elbows close to my side, and my eyes close. *I'm falling.* I lay flat on my back and feel the sharp edges of the leaves prick the side of my face. *I can't move.* Flies buzz around Suzy's head and the blood from her back has dried and thickened into a dark red color glossed like candle wax. There is a plum size hole on her side that must've come from a gun shot. My chest fills with air and it pushes out, again and again. I watch the subtle movements of nature all around me. A slight wind picks up a leaf and it tumbles near my face. The leaf gets caught on the tip of my nose, and I try to lift my arm to flick it away, but my arms and legs won't move. I feel the tiny legs of ants crawling up my leg, but still, I can't move. I take deep breaths like Mama always tells me: 'Relax Sol, relax.' My heartbeats settle; things are quieting now. I can twinkle my fingers and move my feet.

I push myself up. My eyes lock on Suzy in a pained stare. Heat fills my body to a point to where I can do nothing but run back to the house, pumping my legs and arms swiftly, while tears stream down my face. As soon as I get past the last row of trees encasing the woods, I see a streak of dirt rising from the road and I hear a truck engine. I get to the top of the small hill and I can see that it's Pastor William's truck and Mama is in the passenger seat.

60

I cup my hands around my mouth. "Mama," I yell. The truck continues to move along the road. "Mama," I yell again, only louder this time and wave my hands in the air. She swings her head around, and moments later, the truck slows and comes to a stop. The truck doors open, and they both spring out. I sprint to the truck.

When I get close, Mama starts running in my direction while Pastor Williams tapers off, waiting to hear what the whole commotion is all about.

"What's wrong baby?" she screams, with a worried look plastered on her face. She stretches her arms and grabs my shoulder. "What's the matter?"

"That white man den shot Suzy. Suzy dead."

Pastor flanks Mama by a few feet. He flicks a small cigarette to the ground. "He did what?"

"He killed my cow. Shot her dead, and she wasn't even on his side of the fence—not even on his land."

Mama wraps her arm around the top of my back and rubs my shoulder. "It's okay, baby. It's gon' be all right," she says. Her eyebrows furrow, and she looks Pastor directly in the eye. "Take me back home right now."

Pastor shrugs and turns one of his palms at Mama. "Go home?" he asks. "Whatchu wanna go home for? Let's go down yonder and see what's going on."

Mama bites her bottom lip. "I need my shotgun."

He throws his hands up. "Hold, hold...you don't need to get no shotgun about this cow. Let's go on over there and see what he gon' say first."

Mama releases her grip on my shoulder and nudges me to the side of the road. "Wait right here," she whispers through her tight lips.

She walks over to the Pastor, who now leans against the truck, and gets right in his face. Even though she tries to keep me from listening in, I pick up enough words to know that Mama ain't about to have the Pastor just drop her off at work.

"Pastor, you gon' take me home right now...no, no, no...I don't wanna hear it...last time we...ain't nobody gon' walk over us..." she says, pressing her arms down several times to stress her point.

After a few minutes of pleading, Mama turns to me, "Get in the truck." I get into the truck and move to the middle of the hard seat and look over the dashboard that has maps and papers scattered on top. Mama reaches behind the seat and pulls out a short barrel shotgun. "This the only one you have?" she says, standing inside the opened door and staring at the Pastor. He leans into the truck, grabs the steering wheel, and rests his back against the seat.

He takes a sigh before answering. "Yeah. It's the only one I keep in the truck. I keep my Chester at the house. That's the one I used to use fo' most of my hunting. That there in yo' hand, it's just something I keep in the truck. Just in case I see some animal out there and have to protect myself."

Mama holds the gun up and lets her eyes scan the barrel like she's inspecting a precious piece of jewelry. "This just fine fo' me. Do it got some bullets in it already?"

"Two shots. That's all that's in there."

"Okay," Mama says. She pulls the side of her pants away from her waist, pushes the gun down her pant leg, and let's her shirt conceal the gun's handle. She gets back into the truck and yanks the door, *clunk*.

The ride to the white man's house is quiet. Mama raises her

arm and allows her elbow to rest on the interior of the door window. "This it right here," Mama says, pointing to her right. The truck judders over the bumpy road leading to the house. It's a modern style ranch home with a circular driveway. In the center of the circle is a small flower bed filled with yellow and red roses standing proud like service clerks in an exquisite hotel. My palms sweat, and a puddle of sweat forms on my forehead.

The truck comes to a stop. Mama looks through the open window then turns back to us. "Y'all stay here. I'll be right back."

"Now Kat, you know you cain't be going up here and get into nothing with that man. Let me go talk to 'im and see what he say."

"Naw, pastor. I got this one," she says. She pulls on the chrome door handle, gives the door a push with her shoulder to open it, and she heads toward the door. She knocks on the door and no one answers. I'm almost happy no one is here. When she gets back into the truck, she is silent, letting her eyes gaze into the field of green as we take the short trip back to our house.

But I know things won't be the same after this day. I'm thinking about how much different things would be with a dog. He could've kept Suzy on our land or warned me of danger. Suzy is dead now, and I can't bring her back.

CHAPTER TEN

I can't take it no more.

Mama tries to get me to go to school, but I stay home and fiddle around the barn most of the morning thinking about the trap I'm in. When the sun hits, I press my back against an exterior barn wall under the roof hanging to get a bit of shade and allow my body to drop to the ground. *I'm gon' me a dog.*

I look and I see the entry in the woods from a distance and begin flicking rocks into the pasture and watching them disappear in the tall grass blades. The few wispy clouds are cuddled in a massive, blue backdrop. *Is heaven really up there? Does God even care about us?* I hear the creaking of the screen door opening and *thuds* of the door slamming against the door frame in successive sounds that fade away with every...*bluck-bluck-bluck.*

From my peripheral view, I notice Mama walking toward me. She crosses her arms, then immediately uncrosses them, then crosses them again as she gets closer, and holds a cigarette snug between her fingers.

I keep my head pointed forward. She lowers herself and sits next to me.

"You okay?" she whispers. I lean forward and allow my elbows to settle on my knees. She places her hand on my shoulder. "Look son. I'm sorry all this is happening." She puffs the cigarette and blows the smoke out while saying, "I'ma have to Charlie to get up there and get the cow and bury 'im." She drops the cigarette onto the ground and grinds it with her shoe. "That's about all we can do now. But when I see that white man, I'ma pull my shotgun out on 'im and see what he do."

A cold shiver runs up my spine. "You don't have to do that Mama. Why you gon' pull a shotgun out on him? What's that gon' do?" I say.

"What's it gon' do?" she says, frowning.

"I mean, all that's gon' happen is he gon' come back here and try to shoot us or something. Can't we just go to the sheriff and tell 'im he killed our cow?"

"The sheriff?" she chuckles.

"Ain't that's what he for?"

Mama's smile fades quickly and she tilts her head, looking directly at me. "Son, I been tellin' you...white folks don't care nothin' about you. Them people will shoot you down as quick as they did that old cow," she says.

"So, what am I supposed to do?" I say, fuming. "Just stay around the barn and do nothing?"

Mama presses her lips together tightly and stabs me with a cunning stare. Every time she stresses her point, I know she's really talking about me not getting a dog. *I'ma get me a dog though. A full-blooded hound.*

I decide to save my own money to purchase a fine hound dog just like the ones I saw at Furly's. But the only problem is, Mama would never pay $5 for a dog, and I only have a few coins of my own. I decide to change that. On a Saturday morning, I make my way down County Road 42, fighting the scorching heat and swiping my forehead with the back of my hand often to keep the sweat from finding its way into my eyes. I walk from farm to farm, asking if any of the families need some help with farm work or house chores. Most of the families offer me snacks such as peaches and pecans, some even give me cool water from the ice box.

Mama Johnson has seen me in church and knows I am Kat's boy and kin to Charlie. But she says she doesn't need much done in the yard, because she is too old to farm and might need me to come back to help her shell some peas after harvest.

Old man Micah, another elder in Sumerville, calls me to sit down beside him and tell him why I need money so bad. He is a freed slave, who also fought in the First World War, and is popular in town for his unending tales of slavery and war. Though he was only a teenager at the time of Emancipation, he had heard horrific stories from his parents about how his family was ripped apart by the white man.

I know the old man will not offer me work, but I can't find it in myself to be rude and just leave the him talking to himself. I sit beside Micah, who grins and exposes a set of toothless gums that make me flinch both in fright and disgust. He tells me he'll be 100 years old in a few years.

The old man starts his often-repeated story with the very same statement I have heard more than once.

"Say," he says, as one who is singing the first lyric of a very long song, "reckon' you wouldst believe if I tel' ya this here land was a field of sugarcane and cotton, and I saw two men hang from that tree," he points, "for nothin' but eatin' them canes. Just one cane is all they ate. Such a bad, bad time it was." I had heard the story from Mama even before I saw this man for the first time, and I had heard the same story, with the same opening, more times than I can count. He nods quickly and then shakes his head and looks sad. Old man Micah continues to tell me the details of the story while I keep my gaze on the sun which is rising quickly as if it is being pursued. Mama had warned me to return home before noon and to do some work on the farm, and I had promised I wouldn't stay too long at Johnny's; at least that's where she thinks I am. I still have a lot of houses to cover if I am going to get a job before returning home.

For the next couple of minutes, old man Micah left the story of slavery without really finishing it and begins to tell me about how he got drafted for the war as a black man. The sun is almost completely out of the horizon, and I realize noon isn't so far off. But I still don't know how to leave the old man without offending him. *God, please get me out of this.*

It seems the heavens heard my prayer in the form of a hefty, old woman walking past the old man's house who made the mistake of waving her hand to greet him.

"Sara, that you?" The elderly man waves back and calls the woman.

She smiles and comes in our direction. "Yeah, it's me. You ready to getcho daily walk in today?"

"Oh yeah. Just sittin' here waiting for you."

I see an opening and make an escape through a path between the flower garden just beside the front porch. I keep twisting my shoulders around, expecting the old man to call me back, until I am out of his sight completely. I find myself in the front yard of another house, and head straight for the front door. "Good morning," I say to no one in particular as I knock on the door twice. I see a pair of boots on the porch and figure someone must be here. "Good morning!" I say, much louder before knocking again.

"Yes, good morning," the deep voice of a man answers, and the door opens some moments later. "Yes?" the man says. He stares at me and frowns, but I can't tell if he's just pure mad or if he has bad eyes.

"Michael ain't here, youngin'." The man starts to shut the door. "You gon' have to come back."

"I ain't lookin' for Michael, sir," I say. *I don't even know who Michael is.*

"So, what you lookin fer, boy?" The man isn't pleased to have been so rudely interrupted from whatever it was he was doing. He looks down at me and keeps his face tight.

"Lookin' for something to do, sir." The man's face starts to relax. "I can clean your barn or cut that there patch of green you have out there, sir." I point to the grass in the front yard which looks overdue for trimming. A frown quickly returns to the man's face. "Or work in your chicken coop," I interject quickly and expose my white set of teeth. "Anything to help, sir."

The man smiles again, shrugs, and steps out before closing the door after him. "And why you gon' help me on such a fine Saturday morning? I reckon your friends are out playing they boots off in them woods or doing some good fishing, huh?" The man is almost laughing. "What you gon' help me for?" He folds his arms together and waits for me to answer him.

"Oh, yes, sir," I start, "I just wanna help sir. Maybe there's something 'round here I can help you with. And if you find in your heart to give me something, it would be much appreciated, sir."

The man nods. Without saying another word, he leads me to his barn and stretches out his hand toward the door. "Suppose you can start here?"

I nod. "Oh yessir. I can finish this quick, real quick."

The man smiles and starts to leave, then he stops and turns back. "Say, boy, what should I call you?"

"Sol."

"Sol? Like Solomon in the Bible?" He grins.

"Yessir."

The man squints his eyes. "Who yo' kinfolk?"

"My mama name Katherine Canning. People call her, Kat. We live on the second road off from the main road near the post office in Sumerville. Kinda back in the woods."

"Oh. Okay. I know yo' folks. Y'all go to Living Tree Baptist, right?"

"Yessir."

"And Cha'lie yo' kin, right?"

"Yessir. That's my uncle."

The man stands with his hands planted on his waist, then points. "Okay, the broom is in the shed out back, and you'll see my big rake in there too. Don't be meddlin with nothing else in there. Ya hear me?" I stand with a blank face and nod. "If you tidy things up in here, then I'll definitely take care of you."

I gaze at the man until he's inside of the house before setting about my work. The sun is now shining down in full force, though it is still morning. When I open the barn door and look inside, I think about leaving. The barn looks more like the aftermath of a wind and rainy storm than a home for animals and storing feed. The stalls are empty and horse boo boo is scattered all around the barn's floor and this is the only sign that horses once lived here.

Some sections of the barn have fallen in and wood pieces lay all over the place. I drop my head and step outside, thinking about leaving. *I can't do this.* I'm five steps into my journey when images of the puppies I saw in Big Furly's store enter my mind, and I feel a tingling inside just to think about the dogs. I clenched my fists and steel myself before turning back. I narrow my eyes and focus on completing the job at hand. *I'ma get me a half a dollar at least.* I press the sides of my mouth back, grinning from ear to ear.

First, I remove the scattered wood planks and pack them together in a bundle at the back of the barn. I take an old broom standing beside the door and sweep the barn from back to front. Halfway into the work, I remove my shirt, fold and lay it neatly on a chair just outside. It is one of my favorite shirts, and I had worn it because I thought it would make me look smarter and increase my chances of being hired.

Two hours later, the barn is as clean as it could be, and all the broken parts are stacked together at the back. I stand beside the door and look back at what I had been able to achieve in such a short time, and smile to myself again, satisfied. I clap my palms together and dust myself off. *Bet this gon' get me at least a half dollar, maybe a full dollar.* I grin brightly and close the barn's door,

I head back to the house. The man sitting in a rocking chair on the front porch. He is reading a magazine and a jug of lemonade sits on a tray in front of him. Two empty glasses are on each side of the jug and a small plate on the table has some nuts on it.

The man looks up when he sees me approaching. "Boy, you don' already finish the work?" He smiles. "You a good worker, son."

I smile and clasp my hands in front of myself. "Yessir. Thank you, sir. Got it all tidied up like you said."

"Comere." The man picks up one of the empty glasses. "Have some of this cold lemonade." He raises the glass. "It's good stuff... fresh. Came right off my own lemon tree," he adds, as I collect the glass.

"Thank you, sir." I see the small water droplets dangling on the outside of the jug.

The man fills my glass to the brim and smiles. "My name is Benjamin, but you call me Ben, son."

"Nice to meet you, sir." I lift the glass to my mouth and tilt the bottom upward until nothing is left.

Ben laughs. "Told ya it's good stuff. Have another cup." He pours more lemonade into my glass and stops halfway. "You don't wanna drink too much so fast. It'a have you crampin' like something crazy. Trust me."

"Thank you, sir," I say, and take another gulp from the glass.

After a moment, Ben reaches deep into his pocket and pulls out several coins. He cups the coins in the palm of one hand and picks coins with the index and thumb of his other hand. He counts as he separates the coins. "Twenty-five, fifty...seventy..." He stops when he arrives at one dollar and twenty-five cents. My breath stalls, and I'm watching on with serious intent. "One twenty-five.

Is that enough, son?"

"Oh, yessir. That's just fine." I drop the coins into my pocket. "Oh, that'll be just fine. I'll come back."

Ben smiles. "Okay. You take care now."

"Oh. Yes sir. I will. You take care too."

I turn and start a slow jog to the road. When I get to the road, I smooth my shirt and wipe my face with the palm of my hands. Up the road is a heavy-set woman and she is pinning clothes to a line. She has fat cheeks and she recognizes me immediately.

"You Cha'lie kin folk, ain't you?"

"Ma'am?" I say, while squinting.

"Cha'lie."

"Oh, yes ma'am. He's my uncle, ma'am."

"Thought you looked like him. Them eyes just give you away," she says. "Now, Kat is yo' mama, right."

"Yes, ma'am,"

"What brings you here? I see you been up to Ben's house. Ain't seen him actually let nobody in that barn in a long while. Prolly, three-four years since he den had somebody up in there."

My eyes drift from the woman to Ben's house, then back on the woman. "Helped him do a few things. Cleaned out the barn, swept the floor. General straightening, ma'am. That's what brings me down the road. Lookin' to help some folks out. See if I can make a few cents," I say, and the woman's face shifts to display her pity. She smiles.

"Oh. You just as sweet as you wanna be, son. Say you tryna make a few cents, huh?"

"Yes, ma'am. Tryna get me a fine dog all by myself. Wanna train him to be the best coonhound in all of Sumerville."

SOL & SIMONTON

The woman smiles kindly. "If I give you fifty cents—now that's all I have. I want you to promise me that you gon' stay in school and keep ya'self in Sunday School. Ain't nothing out here better than finding yo' place with the Lord. Now, you promise me that and Old Miss Jenson gon' give you fifty whole cents."

I smile and promise to work hard in school and continue to pray. She gives me the shiny silver coins and picks three big oranges from the basket set beside her. "And take these oranges too."

"Thank you, ma'am." I collect the oranges and bow my head in gratitude. "Thank you very much, ma'am," I say. "But I wanna do something for ya..."

"Naw, naw...it's okay, sweetie. Now, run off son before yo' mama start worrying 'bout where you at."

I give her a slight bow again before taking off toward the road.

My arm muscles are taut and my bones feel weak from the hard work I did, but my resolve to get a dog is growing stronger. My feet are too weak to run so I walk instead, with quick and long strides. I don't know what time it is, but I know I must get home as quick as I can.

CHAPTER ELEVEN

I am sitting on a tree stump near the barn drawing designs on the ground with the end of a thin tree branch. This is the first time in a long time that me and Mama missed church. After the man killed Suzy, Mama has been real quiet. I'm taking a rare break from house chores and farm work, waiting for her to leave and go to work so that I can sneak back up the road to make more money. Out of nowhere, I hear footsteps approaching. My eyes dart around, and I tremble. The warning Charlie gave me about the boars and the Klan are fresh in my mind, and my heart beats uncontrollably. The footsteps draw closer. I stand, clench my jaw, and wait. The footsteps then go silent.

Suddenly, I hear the same footsteps draw nearer with increasing speed, and I also hear the heavy swish of a man's pants.

I turn toward the house. "Boo!" A loud voice blares. I freeze in flight and turn slowly. A smiling face looks directly at me. It is Uncle Charlie. He is hitting both of his feet with the end of his walking stick, making the footsteps sound strange and frightening.

"Boy, you shoulda seen yo' face! You was white as a ghost." Charlie laughs loudly and mocks me. "You thought a Hank got you, nephew?"

"No," I say, with a long drag.

"They don't get good boys, don't you worry," he says, leaning on the walking stick, "or do they?" He is visibly enjoying himself, and the look of misery on my face must make him laugh. He has a brown box sitting on the ground next to him. I just stand there, staring at him.

"Is this the way to welcome yo' family?" Charlie asks and walks toward me. "Boy, you dead?"

"Hey, Uncle Charlie," I mumble, "you scared the daylights out of me."

"You don't sound very excited to see me," Charlie notes and his face beams with a big smile. "Where yo' mama at?"

"She in the house," I answer, then lead him across the yard to the house.

Mama is sitting in her favorite chair and knitting. She raises her head when she sees her brother, but she is not particularly happy to see him, and I can tell.

"Look what the wind den blew in," she says, with a snicker. "What brought you to this part of the woods?"

Charlie grins and looks around the house. "Very happy to see you too, Kat," he says, "seems like I ain't been here in months."

"You *haven't* been here in months," Mama says, pointedly with a slight accusation laced in her voice.

"Yeah, I know." Charlie leans awkwardly on his stick. "Ain't easy to walk around on a bad leg." He leans more to the stick side to drive home his point, and he limps forward, showing just how hard it is to walk. "If I can only get a chair to sit and rest this here leg," he says, returning his own tone of accusation to his sister. They go back and forth like an intense tennis match.

I drag one of the chairs across the floor and place it beside Charlie. "Are you okay?" I ask with concern.

Charlie laughs. "Ain't much really wrong with the other leg. Let's just say it's good enough for that good check." He winks and I frown, confused. I don't know if he is joking or serious. Charlie sits, and winces as he stretches out the bad leg. He drops his walking stick on the floor and places the small box on his lap. I smile in self-mockery and take a seat on the floor. It has been a long time since I have seen my uncle come around the house; and the last time he came, he didn't even come inside before he left. I go to the kitchen and get a cup of water for my uncle. Charlie collects it with a big smile and calls me "main man." I smile and think the name sounds good.

"Let's get down to business," Charlie says, with his whole face beaming again. "Main man," he calls me again, "take this box here." He pushes the box away from his body toward me. I take light steps toward him and collect the box. It feels heavier than I expected. I scoot the box up with my thigh to get a better hold of it.

Charlie rises from the chair. "You got it?"

"Yes. I got it, unc."

"There you go," Charlie says, still smiling broadly, "go on now, open it." I gently lower the box to the floor and pull the top flaps back. The bottom of my stomach tingles as I open the box. I hear a groan. Inside, is a tan-colored puppy. I look at my mama, and she looks back with the end of her lips curving ever so slightly with a hint of smile which quickly disappears.

I look back at my uncle and wonder if it's all part of his unending pranks. "It's yours, nephew," Charlie assures me. "He's from a litter of six puppies, and he was the healthiest one in the bunch." I pick up the puppy and slowly raise it from the box. I turn to my mama again, afraid she might object to having a dog in her house. She smiles and even stops knitting for a moment. I pull the puppy's head close to my face, and I see my reflection in his big black eyeballs. The puppy sniffs my hands and laps at my fingers. This makes me laugh; my heart feels lighter, and it's hard to contain my joy. I hold the puppy high in the air and inspect his entire body. There are some small dark spots amidst the tan color. The puppy seems to be in perfect condition.

"Is he full-blooded? Big Furly told me the full-blooded, purebred dogs are the best."

"Ain't no dog out there all the way pure, I tell ya, son," Charlie says. Though I try to hide it, my eyes fall, and I force a smile to hide my disappointment. Charlie looks at Mama and continues. "No dog is completely full-blooded. The doctor who sold the puppy to me told me so. What does old man Furly know about dogs? He ain't nothing but a salesman. He tryna get you to spend a lot of money on a dog." Charlie turns to Mama. "You see how much they charging fo' rice up there at that sto'?"

Mama shakes her head. "Yeah. Ain't no telling. What white folks you know ain't tryna make money off of us?"

"You ain't neva lied," Charlie says, "'sep that time you told daddy you going to the rehearsal and ended up at them white folks' party."

Mama's mouth drops. "Boy, stop lying."

"Oh, yes you did."

I rub the puppy's head, turn, and smile at Mama and Charlie. I love to see them poke fun at each other. Seeing her smile brings a warm feeling in my chest. Mama reaches down for her shoe. "I should take this shoe and throw it at you."

"And I'm gon' be out that do' befo' you let it outta ya hand."

"Yeah. And you pretending yo' leg so messed up. Boy you need to go somewhere wit' that and sit down somewhere." The two laugh. I see a glow in my mother that I don't see often.

When the laughs subside, Charlie looks at me. "This gon' be a fine puppy. He'a grow into a good hunting dog if we train him right," Charlie insists. "The doctor also told me the puppy's father came from a line of German Shepherds used by soldiers during the First World War. There ain't no dog who can beat them Shepherds when it come to loyalty."

I start to smile again, and the puppy happily claws at my chest. "Good puppy, puppy dog," I say and laugh.

"You got yourself a fine dog there, nephew," Charlie says, and presses both hands on his walking stick as he stands.

"I'm grateful, Uncle Charlie. Thanks a lot."

"Thank yo' mama too." Charlie winks at me and walks toward the door with his hat in hand. Just before he exits the door, he turns his shoulders and looks back at Mama. "Don't bother seeing me off, sis. Look like you den let the devil take over all ya spirit."

She breaks a wide smile, picks up a small cup near her chair, and tosses it in Charlie's direction. She had no real intent on hitting him because the cup landed far from his feet. "Now, you get on way from here with that foolishness. Mama always told me you ain't nothing but a fool. You think you so special 'cause you the baby." Charlie laughs it off and pulls his hat snugly onto his head.

"Take care nephew."

"Bye, unc."

Charlie walks through the yard in the direction of the road. He turns back to Mama who is now standing on the porch with her hands on her hips. "That's right," Charlie shoots back. "They say God take care of fools and babies. Last I heard, Charlie ain't no baby." Mama just stands there, shaking her head, grinning, and watching her brother move onto the road and disappear.

When Charlie leaves, I ask my Mama, "Did you and Uncle Charlie get the puppy for me?"

"Go play with your puppy outside, son," she says, and continues knitting.

I drop the puppy back into the box, run to my mother, and hug her tightly around her neck. "Thank you, mama," I say, softly.

Mama stiffens and sighs. "Go play with your dog outside." I loosen my hug, pick up the puppy, and go outside. I stay outside the house with the puppy until the sun goes down, feeding him some milk and small portions of grits left over from breakfast. I made a leash out of rope and an old piece of leather. I let him move around my feet during dinner, and Mama lets it pass for the first day. When Mama retires to her room for the night, I stay in the front room and sit in the chair with the puppy on my lap.

I get on my knees and thank God for my puppy. I also thank God for my mother and Charlie. When the puppy finally goes to sleep, I place him beside me on the bed and put a blanket over his body. I know my life will change forever. I can't wait to go on adventures in the woods with my dog and chase coons, then sell the meat and fur for profit, and have a friend I could care for and always depend on.

CHAPTER TWELVE

I wake to the smokey scent of hickory and hear bacon sizzling away in a hot pan. I push my arms overhead and interlock my fingers, stretching my back and grunting while forcing air out of my chest. Settling my eyes on the foot of my bed, I see my new puppy curled into a ball near my feet. *He's already protecting me.* His coat is a shiny golden color. I rub his head, and he unravels and starts nipping away at my fingers and wagging his little tail.

"Sol. Get on up now. I made some bacon for you today," Mama yells from the kitchen.

"Yes ma'am. Be there inna minute, mama."

I sit the puppy on the floor and start playing with him. I roll a ball across the floor, and he darts after it. Every time he claws for the ball, it rolls farther and farther away from him. When he corners it against the wall, he gnaws on the ball and makes a wimpy growl. I giggle at the puppy's antics. Though he's young, I am impressed at his natural instincts.

"Sol. I'm not gon' call you again."

"Okay, mama. I'm coming."

I wish I could stay home all day with him and start training him, but I have to go to school. So, I might as well get to school and get home as quick as I can so that I can play with him.

I place the puppy in the box and rush to the kitchen. I wash my face and brush my teeth. When I get back to the room, I pick up the puppy and take him outside to pee. I lower him to the ground and he stands next to the first step on the porch and gazes into the open space. He tilts his nose up and sniffs the air, then scampers across the yard in tiny steps to where the red dirt starts to blend with green grass blades. After peeing, he scratches the ground with his paws, then runs back to where I'm standing. I put him back in my room and close the door.

"You like the puppy?" Mama asks, sitting across from me at the table.

"Yes. I love 'im mama. You and Uncle Charlie really surprised me with that." I bite down on a piece of bacon. "This bacon is good mama. Thank you."

"Yeah, I picked some up there at the store. Got us a pound of it. Make sure you take a few pieces to Johnny when you leave."

"Yes, ma'am."

"Now, he ain't staying up in here long. I'll give you two weeks. Then you gon' have ta build 'im a house or put him out there in that barn, but he cain't stay in here. I ain't neva been one to like a dog running around in no house."

"Oh, yes ma'am. I was thinking about building a house for 'im and put it right out there on the other side of the barn."

"That'll be just fine."

"I'll start working on it this Saturday."

Mama gives me a note. "Make sure you give this to Miss Shelby on account you wasn't there last Friday. I don't want her asking me nothing about it during church this Sunday. Everybody already talkin' 'bout that man who shot our cow, and I don't want you sayin' nothin' about it, you hear me?"

"Yes, ma'am."

***

It's misty and the fog blocks my vision, making it almost impossible to see. A blackbird whistles as it flies over my head. I smile, thinking about how my puppy ran to me when I stood by the porch earlier. I take a deep breath and fill my lungs with the smell of morning dew and the wet decaying wood that fills the air. I jump over a large puddle of water on the road and feel a tingle on both ankles as I land back on my feet.

"What? You tryna be in the Olympics or something?" Johnny says from behind a bush near the road leading to his house.

I laugh. "Naw, I didn't know I was gon' land in no water. It ain't like I couldn't jump over it if I wanted to."

"Bet you can't." Johnny says.

"Bet a nickle I can."

"Bet."

"Hold this." I hand my book bag to Johnny, then trot back up the road a few feet and get in position. I rock my body back and take off running. Just before I get to the puddle, I leap into the air and clear the puddle.

"There you go champ." Johnny says, clapping his hands and gleaming with a broad smile.

Johnny hands me my bag, and we start walking. "Told you I could do it," I say, still catching my breath.

Johnny giggles.

"I did it right?" I ask, shrugging my shoulders.

"Yeah. You did it."

"Why you still laughing though?"

"It's funny 'cause you did it when I was watching."

"So, what that mean?"

"It means, somebody was watching."

"Whatever," I say, "aye, I got a puppy yesterday."

Johnny stops in his tracks. "You did?"

"Yep. Uncle Charlie brought him by last night."

"What kind is he?"

"A coonhound-shepherd mix. I'm about to turn him into a champion coon hunter."

Johnny squints. "'A champion coon hunter? What's that?"

"Um...a coon hunter that's a champion, maybe..." I say, with sarcasm.

Johnny stands, dumbfounded. "Oh."

I laugh and nudge him on the shoulder. "Aye, let's go before we're late to school." We jog side by side down the road to school. My face cracks into a smile as my eyes settle on Movery; she also smiles back. "I got a puppy!" I scream, with a voice that is drowned out by the loud noise of other kids. "My Uncle Charlie got 'im for me!"

Movery's eyes brighten up and she smiles back, waiting for me to settle in. "You got it? Is it like one of them coonhounds you seen at Big Furly's?"

"No, my uncle couldn't get one of them," I say, a bit disappointed. But I smile again quickly, "But he got me a good hound. He's mixed with shepherd."

"Heard them shepherds are good dogs too," Movery says. "When you gon' let me see 'im?"

"Mama said I should keep it in the house for a week before he goes out with me. She said it will help him to know the house well, and he'a also know my smell."

"I heard about your cow," Movery whispers.

"Yeah. That man ain't nothing but the devil. Killed my only cow." I drop my head. There's silence.

"You give your dog a name yet?"

I shake my head slowly, "Ain't got no name yet."

"Will you call him Jack?" Movery suggests. "I read of a dog in one of the books my brother has. His name is Jack, and he was a real good dog. He caught some thieves and saved the city," she says, with her eyes beaming. "Call him Jack."

I shake my head slowly. "I don't know..." I say, looking doubtful. "It's a good name though."

Miss Shelby enters the class before I can say more. My classmates muffle their noises, and din quickly ends. I struggle to keep my attention in class. I stare at the rectangular bricks of the classroom wall rather than the blackboard where Miss Shelby is scribbling notes with white chalk. My mind wanders, and I want to know if the puppy is doing okay and not feeling lonely just sitting alone in my room. I turn my head and look through the window. *School, hurry up and end.*

While Miss Shelby stands in front of the class and writes some math problems on the board, I stare at a white paper on my desk and make a sketch of a small puppy. Movery whips her head around, sees me doodling, and taps my desk. I raise my head quickly just in time to see Miss Shelby staring back at me and smiling. I smile back.

"Are you all right, Sol?" Miss Shelby's eyebrows contract. "Are you sick?"

My smile grows wider. "Good and fine, Miss Shelby." I say, a bit too loudly. Miss Shelby frowns slightly and then smiles before she continues with instruction.

It's two hours into class and I'm suddenly flushed with panic, with the strange feeling that the puppy will be dead by the time I get back home. I try to smile and dispel the fear, but the image of Suzy's dead body lying stiff still fills my mind. My palms get warm, and I rub both hands on the front of my shirt. I look around the class. My knees shake, anticipating the end of school.

When school finally ends, I rush out of class before any of my classmates. I'm almost in full stride when I hear Movery's voice. "Aye, where you going so fast?"

I turn back and breathe heavy. Johnny is standing next to Movery. "I gotta get back home. See y'all tomorrow."

The closer I get to the house, the more convinced I am that the puppy is dead. Mama is in the garden, and I greet her quickly, leap onto the porch, and move into the house. I cover the length of the front room floor in a few quick and wide steps and enter my room. I bend forward and gasp for air as I stand before the sleeping dog, smiling and taking a deep breath. I touch the puppy's nose and feel its coldness. He's breathing, and very much alive. I bend at me knees and grin. "Boy, you made me scared for nothing while you laying here sleeping like a rock." I stroke the puppy's body lightly.

SOL & SIMONTON

"Sol." Mama's voice sounds from outside. My heart skips. I feel the fright in her voice. I exit the room and move through the door. A truck is pulling into our yard and Mama's eyes are fixed on it as she walks briskly toward me. "Go get my shotgun." I run back and grab the gun from behind the door to my mother's room. When I return, the truck slows and stops in front of the house. Mama points at me. "Stay in there, Sol."

The white man gets out and walks slowly around the nose of the truck. He's wearing a cowboy hat and a faded plaid shirt. He's the same man that shot Suzy. Mama stares at him.

"Why you here?" Mama says, with her fists clenched, and she's eye-balling the man something fierce. His eyes drift from Mama to me. I stand in the doorway with one hand on the barrel of the shotgun with the butt of the handle on the floor and tucked behind the wall. My chin trembles.

"I hear you come down the road looking for me. You Kat, right?" he says.

Mama gives him a curt nod. "That's what they call me."

"They say you wanted to talk to me about that ole cow that had been coming on my land."

"That's not what I wanted to talk about."

"Oh. I guess they musta been mistaken then. I hear you and some Pastor came up to the house and you got out the truck and came to my door. I reckon you..."

"That's what happened. That's exactly what happened." Mama says, with a mean flare.

The man chuckles. "Now, you den got me confused here..."

"I came to question why you shot that ole cow. He ain't even came over that gate again after Sol fixed the wire on that gate, but there he was, lying dead on our side of that fence."

The man's face reddens. "Now, I told y'all to fix that fence right," he yells, then points directly at me while I'm still standing in the doorway. "I told that boy right there..."

Mama steps closer to the porch. "Wait a minute. You ain't calling that one a *boy*. Now, you get off my property right now." The man's face tightens. "His name is Sol. And that's what you gon' call 'im."

"I don't give a damn what his name is. You just betta not have no more of your animals on my property, or I'ma kill more of 'em and the law ain't gon' do nothing cause they ain't suppose to be on my property no way," he snarls, then starts pointing and stepping near Mama.

Mama swings her head in my direction and extends her hand toward me. "Sol, throw it to me." I toss her the shotgun. Mama yanks back on the fore-end, *chu-chak*. She holds the shotgun diagonally across her chest.

The man comes to an abrupt stop and pushes his palms toward Mama as steady as he can. "Hold up now. Just hold on up..." His voice trembles.

Mama stands firm. "I told you to get off my property, and I ain't gon' tell you again."

"You know you making a mistake by pulling that gun on me, don't you?"

"You ain't the first, and probably won't be the last."

The man walks slowly to his truck, spinning his head around to make sure Mama stays in his view. He gets into his truck and pulls away. Mama watches the truck as it gets back on the road and disappears.

Mama is still fuming. She walks right past me as I'm standing on the porch and places the shotgun behind the door in her room.

I hesitate. "Mama, you still want me to fix the fence?"

"Hell naw. As long as you fixed the wire on there ain't no animals going through there."

"Okay."

"We can save those materials for something else." She walks into her room and slams the door. When I think about what just happened, I feel the hair stand up on the back of my neck. *Will he come after me and my mama?*

CHAPTER THIRTEEN

My puppy gets bigger over the next few weeks, and we haven't heard anything else from that white man. I build a small, wooden cage next to the barn but I'm too afraid to let my puppy stay in there at night, so he still stays in the house with me. I need to train him and make him into a good coonhound.

I slip out of my room and settle on the chair in the living room. The puppy goes down on his backside and sits beside my feet. *I want to get him out into the woods.* Mama is sitting on the front porch and her hands are working thread into a needle when I step out there. I sit opposite Mama, and the puppy sits between us and moves his head from me to her as if he's wondering if the silence would go on forever. "Can I take him for a walk?" I finally blurt. "I want to take him just there in the pasture and back, that's all?"

SOL & SIMONTON

The puppy moves and settles in between my knees. Mama looks at the puppy and sees him wagging his tail. His neck is becoming too thick for the leash.

"Have you swept the barn?" she asks.

"Yes ma'am. I swept the barn, cleaned the stables, and fed the chickens," I reply, and smile.

Mama eyes the axe stuck in a tree trunk in the yard. "Cut us some firewood," she instructs.

I hurry down the porch steps and tie the puppy's leash around the wooden support. He yelps as I walk away from him and stops when I look back.

"Come on now, boy, be quiet. It won't take me long." I glance at Mama, and I see her lips curve into a smile. I swing the axe into the wood and gather several split pieces. When I'm done, I pull the leash from around the post and walk back to the house. "Done, ma'am."

Mama raises her head. "Go get some dog food from the store up the road. It's too late in the day to get to town," she says. "He cain't be eating regular food, he need some dog food. While you there you might as well get us some milk too."

"Yes, ma'am."

"You can take the puppy along with you if you want," Mama says. "You need some money?"

"No, ma'am." I say, grinning from ear to ear. "I have some money already."

I dart into the house and empty the coins from the jar into my hand and run back to the porch.

"Go to the store and head straight back home," Mama says, handing me a few more coins. "You hear me, Sol?"

I jerk my head up and down. "Yes ma'am. To the store and

straight back home. Got it."

I leap off the porch and pull the leash from around the post. "C'mon boy." The puppy sniffs the ground and pulls on the leash. We stay on the shoulder all the way to the store.

When we get to the store, I see a notice posted just outside the door: Coon Hunting Contest - Bring Your Best Coonhound. I smile and get excited about the contest. I hook the puppy's leash around a wooden post and enter the store. Once in, I pick up a small pack of puppy food, a small carton of milk, and go to the counter. Dred is a thin man and with long arms. He stands behind the counter. "Whatchu got there, Sol?"

"Got a pack of food for my new puppy and some milk."

"Aw, I see you got ya'self a puppy there. What's his name?"

My face goes blank. "Well, I don't have a name for him just yet. Just tryna train him up to be a good coonhound."

Dred nods, and shifts his eyes to see through the screen door. "How old is he?"

"Just a few weeks, but he's getting bigger," I say, then ponder. "So, what does it take to get a dog in that contest?"

"Hmmm..." Dred hums, while he tilts his head upward. "First, the dog gotta be registered. He gotta be a coonhound. If not, he cain't be in the competition. We gon' have us a fine time with the hunting contest. Each person will present at least one dog, and they will go into the woods together to find some game and the dog who can tree the most coons will be the winner," Dred says, like he's reciting a script. "There will also be a section for treasure hunting; the dog that can find a treasure out in the woods will also be made the winner." Dred's eyes light up.

I give him some coins. He gives me change and moves away

from the counter. "Let me see what you got." Dred points toward the door. My puppy is staring into the store through the screen door.

I feel proud. "He's a fine one, ain't he?

Dred frowns slightly and a flicker of doubt crosses his face. "Now, that don't look a bit like no full-blooded hound ya got there," Dred says, and looks from the pup to me. He kneels next to the puppy.

I quickly wipe the smile off my face. "Well, does it make a difference if he's full-blooded or not?" I ask, with my palms out.

Dred forces a smile and raises both hands, "Well, no offense. I'm just saying ain't nothing but hounds been in these contests these past years. Only hounds are allowed, not mixed dogs. And your dog definitely looks mixed to me." Dred rubs the hair under my pup's chin. "The other thing, he just a puppy. Dogs in these contests are experienced. They gotta be at least a year old."

I relax a bit. "I am going to train the puppy into the best coon dog ever. You just watch sir." I assure the man with an air of confidence. We walk back into the store. Dred bags the milk and puppy food and hands it to me.

"But can I..." My words are cut short by the a painful yelp and barks of different dogs from the back of the store. My eyes widen immediately when I hear the commotion.

Dred points toward the door. "Your dog..." he starts to say.

I sprint toward the back door. When I get there, I see two large dogs backing off from my puppy. Blood oozes from the side of my puppy's neck, and I drop to my knees beside him. "What happened?"

The puppy wails and rests his head on the ground. A part of his left leg has a bite mark and the puppy can barely lift it. He continues to yelp in sorrow as I stroke his head and whisper into his ear.

Dexter is a white boy who lives on the other side of the creek. There are two other boys with him. One of them yells, "Look at that mutt cry like a little baby!" The other boy points at my puppy and joins in the laughter.

"Damn you! Damn all of you!" *Idiots.* "I hope all y'all burn in hell!" I scream. Tears fill my eyes, and I step in Dexter's direction. Dred opens the store's door and glares at the boys.

"You boys should better move on now." The boys continue to laugh and stroll off and their hounds follow them. "I suggest you move on too and have a look at that dog when you get home." Dred says, just before he disappears into the store and lets the door close behind him. I remove the leash from my puppy's neck, cuddle him into my arms, and wrap the bag handle around my wrist. He's heavier than before but I'm able to carry him all the way home. He yelps, but the wound is not bleeding much.

I head straight for the barn. I rest the puppy on its belly and clean the wound with a piece of cloth and water. When I dab the wound, he gives off a shriek. "Hush now, boy, hush now." I pour water over the wound. He continues to cry with a sharp shrill.

While I'm blowing air from my mouth onto the wound, Mama comes into the barn. She had been washing some clothes beside the house and must've heard the puppy's sorrowful cries. She stands in the barn's doorway and allows her eyes to adjust to the darkness inside.

"Step back, Sol!" she yells. "Whatchu doing?"

I stand up and take a step back. "He's hurt," I mumble.

"What happened to 'im?!" she asks and looks at the puppy lying on his side.

I rub my wet hands against my chest. "Some dogs attacked

him."

Mama frowns. "What?" She's perplexed.

I look down and stammer, "I tied him to a post next to the store and two of them white boys' dogs attacked him. His poor cry made me run out of the store, but before I got there, they had bit his neck, and bit his leg." My voice quivers, and I feel blood pumping fast through my head.

Mama's face is immediately flushed with anger, and she bites her lip to stop from cursing. "Why you leave the dog by hisself?" She couldn't hide the anger from her voice.

I shrug my shoulders. "I dunno."

"Run into the house and go get me some thread and a needle." Mama bends over the dog. "And the black bottle in the box," she shouts as she cleans the neck wound.

I return with the items and the bottle and drop them beside Mama. I also get a bowl of water and place it on the floor.

Mama opens the bottle and the strong smell of iodine solution fills the air. "This will sting him. Hold him steady and stroke his head," she instructs. "Hold him steady," she says again, and pours some of the iodine on the neck wound.

The puppy yelps in pain, scratches the floor with his paws, and tries to get up. I hold him steady and continue to stroke both his head and legs.

"Sol." I hear Johnny's voice.

"I'm in here," I yell.

Johnny takes slow steps into the barn. "What happened?"

Mama stays focused on the puppy. "Now, I gotta to stitch up that neck wound." She picks up the needle, pours the iodine solution on it, and starts stitching up the cut on this neck. The puppy kicks and scratches more while Mama moves the needle in and out of his flesh, but a few minutes later, it's over. Mama tilts the bottle and pours the iodine over the stitched wound, then rubs her hands into the cloth. "Now, let him rest," she says, "And feed him once he wakes up."

"Thank you, mama," I say, with my eyes still fixed on the puppy.

Mama stands and looks at the puppy as it lays with both eyes half-closed. "He may run some fever. Keep 'im here in the barn. It's too hot outside."

"Thank you, ma'am." Mama closes the barn door.

"What happened to 'im?" Johnny asks.

"Dexter dogs attacked him at the store."

"What? They are complete imbeciles."

"Rest, boy, rest and be strong," I whisper into the puppy's ear and touch his forehead ever so lightly with a wet cloth. "You strong, aren't you? You a strong hound." *Don't die on me.* "Watch, I'ma make him the best hound anybody ever seen in Alabama."

"The whole state?" Johnny asks.

"Yep. All of Alabama."

The puppy winces and raises his head before falling back to sleep. He goes from warm to hot and the fever is not letting up. *Damn this fever.*

"Aye, Sol. I gotta talk to you about something," Johnny says.

"Yeah, what is it?"

"I wanted to come by to tell you we gotta move again."

"Y'all moving? Why?" I ask, if adding to the pain I'm already feeling throughout my body wasn't enough.

"I dunno. We gon' move to Beatrice with my aunt. My mama didn't want to, but we gotta go."

I'm speechless. If seeing my puppy fighting for his life isn't enough, knowing Johnny is moving is a sign that it really does pour when it rains.

CHAPTER FOURTEEN

The end of summer is quickly approaching. My dog beat the fever and has grown to nearly sixteen inches in height and his head has fattened. I haven't spent much time with Movery, and with Johnny moving away and only seeing him at church ever so often, I've been training my puppy every day. Today, I get up late and walk around the porch expecting to see him sniffing around the yard on a scent like he's always doing, but he's nowhere in sight.

"Come on, boy!" I look around and see no signs of the dog. "You over there in that barn, boy?" I walk to the barn. "Come on here boy."

There is silence, no barks. I wonder if he's in a deep sleep and can't hear me. When I get to the barn, I check the outside first. I bend and trace the side wall to see if there are any signs of the boars. There are scratches in the wood and mud smeared on a side wall. "Damn boars!" I yell, swing the barn door open, and go straight to the chicken coop. I hear the chickens cooing, and I heave lightly.

I move around the outside of the barn and see paw prints embedded in the mud. They are too large to be the dog's, and they go directly to the barn door. Beside the large paw prints are the tracks of another smaller paw. I reach my hand into the large claw print. *Boars?* I fix my eyes on the tracks and follow the prints from the barn, and they go clear into the pasture. I stop just behind the low fence and place one of my palms on the post. I look back at the house before I leap over the fence and spring into the woods. My feet get tangled in wiry vegetation, and I tumble forward covering my head during the fall and rolling several times until I come to a stop. I sit up and cup my hands around my mouth. "Where you at boy!" I call out and stand before continuing through the woods. The tracks disappear in the shrubs, and I keep walking, hoping to hear his deep bark. Two red-tailed hawks perch on a hickory tree branch that stands alongside the shortleaf pines running into the woods.

The early morning sun filters through the trees, and I keep moving and calling for my dog. "Come on, boy," I yell, and my voice echoes back to me. When everything falls silent again, I listen hard for a bark, and I hear nothing. Even the hawks on the hickory tree keep quiet. A small squirrel jumps into my path and turns sharply when he sees me approaching. "Come on, boy! Where you at?" I run farther into the woods and the bristles and thorns scratch my elbows, but the rush of adrenaline keeps me moving. I continue running for another few minutes before my ribs start to ache and my muscles grow hot as if on fire. I stand near a big tree with large branches and leaves, and gasp for breath. I sit under the canopy of the branches. "Come here boy!" I shout with every last ounce of my strength and wait in hope for a response. But the silence is loud, and the woods shout my words back to me.

Tears slowly fill my eyes and my lips start to shake. I look around the woods and try to blink back the tears but fail as they flow down my cheeks. An army of red ants march under the cover of a leaf but when I see them, I just turn my face away and sniff. And then, like the sudden rush of heavy rain, tears stream freely down my face and my shoulders shake as I weep like a baby. The pain in my ribs stab at the side of my body, but the ache I feel in my heart is more serious. I squat, bringing my knees close to my chest and drop my head. The light breeze in the woods is cool, and the sound of crickets and smell of the soil soothes me until I doze off.

I wake to the feeling of wetness across his cheek. I blink and wonder how long I've been asleep. My neck aches and I shake myself awake. *It's my dog.* He stands before me panting with his tongue out and his tail dancing in the air. "Where you been!" I cry in pure joy and hug him. The dog rests his front paws on my chest and licks my ear. "Oh boy, I thought I lost you," I whisper and draw the dog closer. The dog buries his head deeper into my chest and laps at my face happily. "Boy, am I glad to see you," I say. "I know you was protecting them chickens. I know what you did, boy," I praise him. "You chased off them boars." I raise the dog's head and bring his face before mine. I stare into the dog's eyes, "Thank you, boy. Thank you." A bird wails loudly from the distance, and a swarm of bees buzz through the woods as I stand. But as much as I love nature's beauty, it is my dog that's putting a smile on my face in this moment.

"Let's go home, boy. Mama gon' be worried." The dog leads the way, and I follow behind him.

CHAPTER FIFTEEN

By the end of fall, the dog's shoulder muscles are thick, his torso is long, and he has two, dark brown circular patches along the base of his back. At only four months old, I know he is too young to start hunting, but it is the perfect time to start training him to tree coons. I have one goal and one goal only, and that's to make sure he only knows how to hunt for coons. I don't want him running deer or rabbits, because he would follow them onto a road or a trap and get himself killed. Treeing a coon seems much safer, but I also know that coons would fight back, and I want him to be ready.

Charlie honks the truck's horn as he pulls up near the house. I leap off the porch with a wide smile and sprint to the barn to get the dog. "Uncle Charlie!" I holler, as I zip past the truck.

"Hey now," Charlie yells back.

Mama is bending and picking up fallen pecans from the yard. She forces a smile, pressing one side of her mouth back.

"About time," Mama says, while walking slowly toward the truck.

I run to the back of the truck with the dog on a leash.

Charlie grins. "Well, maybe if you smile a lil mo'...maybe I'a come visit ma big sister more often."

"Hush up, boy," Mama snaps back. "You always got something to say. If it wasn't for that dog, I probably wouldn't see you 'til the next revival." Mama shoos him with her arm and giggles. "So, you taking him up to cut'n Willie he sayin'?"

"Yeah. You know cut'n Willie 'bout the best one 'round here that know about them dogs. Hunting dogs, house dogs, mutts, coonhounds—he know it all."

"Yeah. Since we was kids that's all he ever talked about." Mama's hand shields her eyes from the sun. "How ole Willie doing anyhow?"

"He don't do much. After Annie Mae died, he mostly stay there around the house. Doing a little fishing, fixing around the house— that's about it."

Mama taps the hood of the truck. "Hey, you want some pound cake? I made one yesterday and it's so moist it'a melt in ya mouth." Mama takes quick steps back toward the porch.

"I knew I came by here for something," Charlie yells through the passenger window of the truck. "Hey, you make it like mama used to make it? 'Cause if it ain't..."

Mama turns and give Charlie a playful stare. "Hmm," she sighs, and places her hands on her hips. "Look boy. You want some cake or not?"

SOL & SIMONTON

"Yeah I want some cake. You think I den went crazy or something?" Mama can only shake her head and grin at Charlie as she turns and goes through the door of the house.

I try to lift the dog onto the back of the truck.

"Wait a minute...wait a minute." Charlie says. He reaches over, grabs his cane, and limps to the back of the truck. "Let me help you get this bad boy up. He bigger than most adult dogs around here." Charlie glances at the dog. "Ooh wee. Whatchu been feeding 'im?"

I shrug my shoulders. "Just regular ole dog food from sto', that's all."

We lift the dog onto the tailgate of the truck, and he scurries his legs under him to get his balance. The screeching sound of his scraping claws against the metal truck bed sends a jolting chill up my spine. I jerk my head and cover my ears with my hands.

"You okay, nephew?" *I didn't think Charlie saw me.*

"Yeah. I'm okay."

Charlie giggles. "Yeah. That sound used to get me too. You'a get used to it." Charlie slams the tailgate shut.

"I'ma stay back here with him, okay unc?"

"No problem with me. Jump on back there."

I hop into the bed of the truck and sit with my back against one of the sides. The dog sprawls himself between my legs with his head resting over my thigh.

"Here you go my loving brother," Mama says, with a pinch of sarcasm. She passes Charlie a small plate covered with a napkin.

Charlie leans against the truck and pulls the napkin back. He breaks a piece of the cake off and pushes it into his mouth. "Umm umm umm," Charlie says, lowering his eyelids and shaking his head. "Girl, you den put yo whole foot in this one. And you gave me nearly a half a cake here."

Mama grins. "Oh wait." Mama turns to the house again. "I got somethin' else for you." When she returns, she passes Charlie two small, brown paper bags. "Fresh pecans. Give one to cut'n Willie, bless his heart...and you take one."

"Girl, seem like I den died and went to Heaven."

Mama taps him on the shoulder. "Now, get on outta here," she says, then points at Charlie. "You betta have my boy back here befo' dark too."

Charlie gets back into the truck and slams the door shut. "I'll have him back whenever you want if I can get some more of that cake."

Mama smiles, then walks near the bed of the truck. "Now, you don't be standing up in the back of this truck when he driving, hear me?"

"Yes ma'am."

"And don't you be letting him keep you out all night. If it get too late, you tell Willie to bring you on up that road, okay?"

"Yes, ma'am."

"'Cause you know how ya uncle can be."

Willie lives up the road from Charlie in a white house with a tin roof. Charlie pulls his truck in a spot right in front of the house. I hear dogs barking from different areas of the property. A Bluetick comes from under the house. A Redbone peers from around the septic tank, comes forward, and starts nipping at the back of the truck trying to jump high enough to see my dog. My dog moves from between my legs and stands. His tail wags and the hairs on the back of his neck stand up like soldiers at full attention.

Willie sits on the front porch, and he's shirtless. He is a dark man and has a cigarette dangling from his mouth and it's slanted across his chin.

Charlie lifts his leg over the running board on the truck and balances himself with his cane. The dogs come running at Charlie. "Now, you get any closer to me and Imma knock you upside the head with this cane. You better move on now."

Willie laughs. "Boy, you better not hit my dogs. They doin' exactly what they 'pose to be doing."

The Redbone charges toward Charlie and growls when he is close to Charlie's leg. Charlie raises the cane and swings it in the dog's direction. The dog doesn't budge. He stands his ground and growls more, showing his canines.

Charlie stares at the dog. "Take one more step, and I'll send your red butt to doggy heaven."

After a fierce showdown, Willie yells, "Hold boy, comere." The dog quickly retreats, runs toward the porch, and lowers himself right next to Willie. Willie pats him on the head. "That's right. You did good, girl. You did good."

"Yeah. She was about to get a good whack right upside her head too."

Willie steps off the porch and takes a slow pace to the back of the truck. "Who we got here?" His teeth have brown stains, and he has a huge gap between his two front teeth.

"This hear is Kat's boy, Sol," Charlie says.

"I know who Sol is. He kinfolk. How you doing cut'n?"

"Fine, cut'n Willie."

Willie squints. "Now, I thought your name was Simon."

"Simon is my first name, sir. But everybody call me by my middle name, Sol. It's short for Solomon."

"Umm hmm," Willie hums, "now, who you got here?"

"This my dog. He's only four months old, and I reckon this is the best time to start training him to be a good coonhound."

"Coonhound, huh?"

"Yessir."

"Whatchu know about a good coonhound?" Willie chuckles. "Whatchu tryna get? Coon meat, felt...fur for yo' mama?"

I turn my palms out and ponder. "Well, we can definitely use the meat, and I can sell the skin. Mainly, I'm just looking for a good hunting dog."

Willie nods his head. "Umm hmm. Now, that skin can get you good money," Willie says, then points to his Redbone hound. "She treed like six coons last time I took her out there in them woods. She be on they tail and won't let up 'til she get 'em up that tree. Now, that Bluetick, she getting kinda old, and she stay close to me. But when she hear that Redbone sing—she gone, boy," Willie taps his hands. "She find the Redbone and they get on 'em. I come along, look up in that tree with the light to see them beady eyes on that coon, get that Chester and pop 'em real good."

"You kill 'em?" I asks.

Willie chuckles, pulls the cigarette from his mouth, and blows smoke through his nose. "That's when the fun come in. Most of the time them coons still alive and that's when your hounds gotta take care of the rest. That's when they have they fun. It don't make no sense that I get all the fun. And them dogs there be knowing it. They want a piece of the action too." Willie reaches and rubs my dog's head, surveys his ears, and looks into his mouth. Charlie and I watch on. Willie pulls on his tail and feels under his throat.

"Whatchu think?" I ask, feeling anxious and excited at the

same time.

"Probably got some English hound in 'im, but not much. Definitely some shepherd. As far as hunting coons, he ain't gon' have that keen sense of smell like them full-blooded coonhounds got, but he might be a okay hunting dog."

I drop my chin. "Why you don't think he gon' be a good coonhound?"

"Ain't saying that cut'n." Willie glances at the Redbone. "That one there is one hundred percent coonhound. Ain't no questioning that. She can go out there and get on a trail quick, but that ain't the only thing that make her a good coonhound. She gotta have some guts to get out there on that trail and not make no mistakes."

My eyebrows contract. "Whatchu mean by that?"

"What I'm saying is...if you want a coonhound, he can't be chasing any ole thing out there. He gotta be chasing coons—that's it. When he get hot on a trail, you don't want him bawling at some ole cat or some ole squirrel up in that tree, you want him to be on a John Brown coon up there."

"How you get 'em to do that?"

"It's all in the training. You gotta train 'em right. Charlie came by here a few months ago and said you was looking for a coonhound puppy. I told him I ain't got no puppies 'cause I just ain't got the time to raise 'em no mo', so I sent him up there on the ridge to get a puppy from a man I know up there. People 'round here want so much money for a full-blooded coonhound. Man, I tell ya', they can cost you some real money." Willie pats the dog on the head. "So, looks like you got you a mixed breed, but he'a be a good dog for you for now. Maybe later on you'll get yo'self a good full-blooded hound."

"I want him to be the best," I say in an elevated tone.

"I'll he'p you get 'im right. He's a big boy. Looks like he gon' weigh a ton."

Charlie looks on and smiles. "That's it."

Me and Willie move our eyes to Charlie. "What dat?" Willie says.

"Simon-ton."

My face goes blank and my jaw drops. "That's it, Uncle Charlie. Let's call him Simonton."

Willie's face spreads to a grin. "Sol and Simonton."

Willie opens the hatch. "Okay. Let's get him off this truck and train 'im up a lil bit."

Simonton jumps off the back of the truck and runs directly to the other dogs. They chase each other around the yard, jumping on each other playfully and pretending to fight. We watch on.

After several minutes, Willie makes his way to the porch and comes back with a folded newspaper. Simonton jumps on the back of the Bluetick and the Bluetick twists his body quickly. Simonton rolls over on his back and the Bluetick growls and snaps at Simonton.

"Don't do that!" I yell.

"Naw. Let 'em play. He'll get used to it," Willie says.

We stand and watch every move the dogs make. Willie opens the newspaper. "So, Charlie, whatchu think about us black folk fighting in that war? Don't seem like we should be fighting a war that don't mean nothing to us."

Charlie hawks and spits onto the red dirt. "You ain't sayin' nothing. All they gon' do is keep us po and broke so we don't do nothing but what they want us to do, and that's to work and fight for them—that's it. Seem like that's just how the world works."

SOL & SIMONTON

Willie's eyes move to the newspaper clutched in his hand. "I guess they think we gon' be happy just because they let us get up there in them planes and fly. So, we 'pose to feel like every thang okay."

Charlie chuckles. "Yeah. We can do all we want up there in that sky. We can fly through the clouds, drop bombs…damn near get to heaven. But when we come back down here, we ain't bit mo' betta than a dog to white folk." The two men giggle.

"You right about that," Willie adds.

Willie tosses the folded newspaper from one hand to the other, then motions with his hand for me to follow him. "C'mon here." Willie walks to an open area near a large tractor. "Aha Aha Aha," he yells out. The Bluetick and Redbone dart to Willie. Simonton sees the two dogs and follows suit. Willie rests his back against the tractor. "The first thing you gotta train yo dog to do is listen to your voice. If he don't listen to yo' command, he ain't gon' be no good dog. He gon' be worthless, not worth a red penny," Willie's eyes follow his dogs, "these here listen to everything I say. If I tell 'em to sit, they sit. If I tell 'em to come here, they come. So, you gotta get yo' dog to do the same thing. When you out there in them woods late at night, all y'all got is each other. He depend on you, and you depend on him. That's the way it gotta be. But if he don't listen to you, you might as well be out there in them woods by ya'self."

Willie shows me several commands. I practice showing Simonton how to sit, lay down, stand, and come to me. Willie uses the newspaper to reinforce the commands. "If he don't act right, you gotta whack him real good wit' that newspaper. That's the best training tool you'a ever have. Pretty soon, he'll obey you and you don't have to use that newspaper no mo'. He'll understand if he get out of line, he'll remember all the times you put that paper to his goddamn head. You understand?" I nod.

Willie demonstrates with the Redbone and Bluetick and they humbly comply. I try several times with Simonton, and he pays me no mind. I tap him on the top of head with the newspaper.

"You gotta hit him harder than that," Willie says, then he flings the cigarette onto the ground. "Let me show you." Willie snatches the newspaper from my hand and moves in close to Simonton. "Sit...sit." Simonton doesn't sit. Willie snaps at him twice with the newspaper and whacks him on the top of the head. Simonton wags his tail and continues standing. "Sit. Sit!" Willie yells once more, this time much louder. He pops Simonton on the head again then pushes his butt to the ground. This time, Simonton looks over at me and eases down slowly. "Now, it don't he'p if I'm the one telling him to sit. You gotta be the one. You his master, and he should only be listening to your voice—nobody else voice."

We work the dogs for another hour. Simonton responds to some commands, but he still needs a lot of work. I'm tired. Simonton lays flat on the bed of the truck and watches every move I make. Whenever I adjust my sitting position, Simonton moves closer to my side then lies back down, never taking an eye off me. I wonder what he's thinking? This is the first time I had yelled at him and hit him with something. I know it's important for him to be obedient, but I didn't realize how difficult it would be for me to punish my dog in order for him to comply.

When we get home, Charlie pulls on the handle to release the hatch and Simonton jumps down from the bed.

Charlie stands near the bed. "Nephew, looks like there's a paper on the front door. Go see what it is."

SOL & SIMONTON

I walk to the porch, pull the paper from the door, and unravel it as I return to to the truck.

"What is it?" Charlie asks, with his forehead wrinkling.

"Some type of letter," I say. I hold the letter in front of me, and read aloud:

> Dear Sol,
>
> The sheriff came by to pick up your mother. Stay with Charlie until she gets back.
>
> Pastor Williams

I turn to Charlie. Everything goes silent. Though I can't see inside his head, I feel tension building. *My mama is in jail.* My heart drops like a huge boulder.

CHAPTER SIXTEEN

Charlie pulls the gear shift lever down and presses his heavy foot on the gas pedal. The truck tires grind into the gravel as he yanks the steering wheel to his left, and the truck shoots forward like a rocket. This all feels like a dream, and I want it to end. We have to get Mama out of jail.

He pulls onto the road. The truck engine roars and the wind whisks through the side window while day dances with night and creates a big splash of gray light over the western sky. I turn my head ever so slightly. Charlie is leaning forward and he says nothing to me. Sweat puddles form just above his temple and he just keeps fiddling with that gear shift and pulling it down. The engine moans like a prolonged yawn signaling the end of an afternoon nap.

He lets his foot off the pedal and we ease into a long curvy turn. When we come out of the turn, he clutches and shifts gears again, and the truck rolls without Charlie giving it more gas. He pulls off the road and moves along a dark, dirt road. All I see ahead are green shrubs cut back neatly on both sides and flattened, red dirt illuminated by the truck's headlights. When we get to the end of the road, Charlie slows and kills the engine. I can see underneath the farmhouse, because it's supported by brick columns spaced a few feet apart with an enclosed porch encased in screen material. The glowing eyes of a cat look directly at us. The cat zips away and silence is replaced by explosive howls from dogs as they encircle the truck.

A light flickers from the inside of the house. Charlie nudges the door with his shoulder, and it opens slightly with a crying squeal. "Getcho butt back," he yells, poking his head into the cracked space. He then slams the door shut and plants his eyes on the house. "Pastor Williams betta come out here and get these mutts before I start knocking them upside they head with this goddamn cane." Charlie says, with bulging eyes and his chest nearly touching the steering wheel.

Pastor Williams steps from the porch. He's wearing a long robe and places his hand just above his forehead palm down to block to glare from the headlights. "Charlie?" he yells, figuring he's familiar enough with the truck to know it belongs to my uncle.

Charlie turns the crank on the side door and sticks his head through the window. The barks intensify. "Yeah. It's me."

Pastor Williams motions toward the truck. "Get back," he reprimands the dogs, swinging his arms at them like a choir director signaling the end of a gospel selection. "Get outta here." The dogs retreat to the bottom of the house.

Pastor Williams continues to the driver's side window. "So, y'all got the letter I left?"

"Yeah. Them fools den locked her up, huh?" Charlie says, keeping his lips tight.

Pastor Williams shrugs his shoulders. "Yeah. You know how they are. Saying she pulled a gun on that white man and threatened to kill 'im."

"She ain't threaten him," I say, scooting up in my seat, "he came on our property talkin' 'bout how he was gon' kill some more of our animals, and Mama told him to get off our property. I threw her the gun, but she ain't tried to shoot that man. He lyin'. He had a gun too, in his holster."

Pastor Williams dips his head and looks directly at me. "Yeah. It don't matter sometime, son. The devil is always working, trying to get us to do evil, and we gotta know just what the Lord want us to do. 'Cause he the one controlling all this, not man."

Charlie grips the steering wheel and turns his head to Pastor Williams. "Ain't no time fo' that kind of talk right now, pastor. With all due respect. We gon' go down there to that jail and get her out. They ain't keeping my sister in no jail. She cain't deal with that. Now, you can go with us or not, but we going."

Pastor Williams pauses. He stares at Charlie then shifts his eyes to me. "Lemme get my coat." He taps the interior of the window with an open palm. "I'a be right back."

When we pull up to the sheriff's station, there's a glass door with Sumerville County Sheriff painted on it in big gold letters, and there's a light on in the building and I see a desk inside the glass doors on the opposite side of the room. Pastor Williams is carrying a worn Bible, and his arms are trembling. Charlie knocks on the door.

"There's the deputy right there behind that desk. I guess he gon' act like he don't see us," Charlie says. I turn and glance at the truck, knowing it's not that far away just in case we have to run. Pastor twists his body, following my gaze. And when I turn back to the door, he does the same.

"Maybe they ain't here," Pastor Williams says. "Maybe we can just come here in the morning."

"Don't you see the deputy sitting behind that desk there?" Charlie spats. "He gon' just act like he don't see us."

Charlie knocks on the door again; this time it's more like a bang than a knock. "You gon' open this do' or what?" He says, much louder than the first time.

I didn't see the man sitting behind the desk when Charlie mentioned it at first, but a large man appears from behind the desk. He's hefty with a huge stomach that spills over the front of his pants and held back by a tightly pulled belt. When he walks, his arms flap high in front of him and his face is the pinkest that I have ever seen. He turns the lock on the door and pulls the door inward without taking his hand off the bar. He tilts his head back and flares his nostrils. "Whatchall want?"

Pastor Williams starts. "Sir, we here…"

Charlie raises an arm to Pastor Williams. "Wait. Wait a minute." He then turns to the man. "Deputy Jolston, right?"

"That's me."

"Charlie Canning."

The fat man blows wind out of his nose and raises his chin high. "I know who you are."

"So, I guess you know why we here?" The man gives Charlie a long, single nod. "I'm here to pick up my sister, and we ain't leaving without her."

The man chuckles. "You ain't leaving without her?"

"That's what I said," Charlie says, with no hesitation.

The man stares at Charlie, pushes the door shut, and flicks the lock. He rolls his sunken eyes and turns away, heading back to his desk.

"That's okay." Charlie mumbles, looking through the glass door at every move the man makes. After a minute or two, Charlie turns to me and Pastor Williams, "Let's get in the truck."

Pastor Williams and I settle into the truck. Charlie stands with the driver's side door ajar, reaches behind the seat, and pulls out his shotgun. He adjusts himself in his seat with the shotgun straddled between his legs, then adjusts his rearview mirror. "We'a just wait here. Ain't nobody coming up in here and taking my sister away." He pulls the top of his hat over his eyes. "I'ma doze off for a minute. If y'all see something wake me up."

"Okay," Pastor Williams says. "I'll stay up and make sure nothing happens."

There's nothing but silence except for Charlie's snoring. My neck is sweaty, and I'm scrunched between the two men. Pastor Williams stares out into the dark sky with his elbow planted on the interior of the window opening and his chin is resting in his palm.

I wonder what he's thinking.

He starts humming familiar tunes that I either hear at church, or hear Mama humming as she's cleaning around the house or hanging up clothes on the line. We're so tight that I feel Charlie's diaphragm buzz against my arm.

"You read yo' Bible, son?" Pastor says, still looking out into the sky.

"Yessir. Every day."

Pastor Williams turns his head and looks forward. "What it mean to you?"

"Well, I...it means like...God can speak to you through the Bible. It's his word."

Pastor Williams smiles. "Okay. So, you sayin' God speaks to you through the Bible?"

"Yeah. I guess you can say that. Yessir."

"You ever read Psalms ninety?"

"I have, but I don't like...remember it."

Pastor Williams presses his thumb against the edge of the pages in the Bible and they cascade down. When he finds the right page, he lowers his head and moves his index finger across the page. "Oh, here. Read this one."

"Verse fourteen?" I ask.

"Yeah. Read that one."

I read the scripture. "Satisfy us in the morning with your unfailing love, that we may sing for joy and be glad all our days."

Pastor Williams' lips press way back on his face and he nods. "See there?" he says, "it says the Lord will 'satisfy us in the morning with unfailing love, that we may sing for joy and be glad all our days.'"

Tears fill my eyes. *I miss my mama.*

Pastor Williams turns to me. "It's gon' be all right, Sol. Yessir, it's gon' be all right."

I rub the tears from my eyes with the back of my hand. Pastor Williams closes the Bible.

"Now, you go on and close your eyes. I'll stay up and watch out. Yo' mama gon' be okay."

I'm dozing off.

I feel nudging on my side. "Get up. The sheriff is coming," says Pastor Williams. "Cha'lie, get up."

Light is breaking through darkness. Charlie pulls up his hat and scoots up in the seat. "Hold this." He moves the shotgun from between his legs and lowers it horizontally near my feet. I feel the cool steel against the front of my lower shin.

Charlie pushes the door with his shoulder. The sheriff's car pulls next to the truck, and the sheriff gets out of the car.

"Morning, Charlie," the sheriff says.

"Morning, Sheriff," Charlie greets back. The two men stand near the front of the sheriff's car while the Pastor Williams and I watch from inside the truck.

Charlie starts talking. "Look, we ain't never had no problems with nobody 'round here. This man only been here fo' two years and he causing all kinds of problems with people. Ma nephew there had a lil ole cow and them boars cut right through the fence, and the cow ain't know no betta, so he went on the man property—ain't no reason fo' him to just up shoot the cow. And when he shot him, the cow was on ma sista land. Now, you and I both know that ain't right, Sheriff."

The sheriff drops his head, then looks in my direction. "Is that your nephew there?"

"Yeah. That's him."

The sheriff walks to the open passenger side window and looks inside. His eyes are blue, his face is skinny, and he has silvery hair around his face just like an old goat. He nods his head and says, "Pastor Williams," before sliding his eyes to me.

"Morning, Sheriff," Pastor Williams replies.

I haven't spoken to many white men before except for Furly

at the store. I feel my heart thump in my chest.

"What's your name, son?"

"Solomon, but everybody call me Sol."

"Good morning, Sol."

"Good morning."

"You wanna tell me what happened?"

"The whole story?"

"Well, just the part when the man came to your house."

"So, this man was mad because our cow went on his land. He killed the cow...me and my mama called her Suzy."

"Uh-huh."

"So, Pastor Williams took me and my mama over there to talk to the man, and he wasn't home. So, a few days later he came to our house and started yelling at my mama. He even had a gun in his holster. So, my mama had her shotgun and just told the man to leave."

"So, that's the whole truth?"

"Yessir."

"Did ya mama ever point the gun at the man or say she was gon' shoot him?"

"Nosir. She never done that or said she was gon' shoot that man."

The sheriff drops his head and ponders. "Okay." He looks back at Charlie. "Comere Charlie." He and Charlie turn their backs to us and whisper. After a few moments, the sheriff goes through the glass doors while Charlie stands just outside the door.

What seems like hours, is only a few minutes. Mama walks out the door. My eyes widen and a huge smile spreads across my face. Mama stomps to the truck. Pastor Williams swings the door open and I leap out and hug my mama tightly. I bury my face into her chest and tears flow freely.

"I'm so happy to see you, mama."

Mama rubs the top of my head. "It's okay, baby. Let's get outta here." She scoots into the center position. "Come on here, boy. Sit on my lap."

Mama is still fuming. "I thank y'all for getting me out, but you shoulda just let me stay in there. 'Cause if that white man come on my land again, I'ma shoot 'im dead. And I ain't playin'." That is all Mama has to say to cause complete silence in the truck. The sun is coming up. It's about to be a hot day.

CHAPTER SEVENTEEN

In the days that follow, Mama doesn't mention anything about being in jail. All I know is, she checks behind her bedroom door several times throughout the day to make sure her shotgun is still there.

On a bitter, cool night, I am awakened by Simonton's loud and ferocious barks. I rush out of bed, pick up the lantern, and put on my boots before running outside. The barks become fainter as seconds pass by. *He must've hit the woods, and I have to get him before Mama comes back home from work.* I don't have a lot of time to find him. The worst of the storm is near, and I hear the loud thunderclaps from a good distance away, but the crushing sounds are getting closer every second. I race to the woods in the direction of Simonton's bark, hoping that he would respond to my call, "Aha-

Aha-Aha." Whenever Simonton gets hot on a trail there isn't much that can distract him from capturing his target. He's like a raging bull. I know he wouldn't back down to anything, even the vicious boars with their long sharp teeth, and that scares me. I know he would fight to the bitter end.

"Simonton!" I yell, as I get to the steep decline on the bank of the creek. I balance himself on a slippery rock. Simonton's bark quickly fades away. The storm raged on. Lightning bolts sizzle through the sky, and the rain pours fiercely. I am smothered in darkness. I twist my upper body, looking in all directions, but the downpour makes my vision misty, and I can't see much through the thick, grayish streams of hail falling around me and crashing onto the ground.

I hold the lantern high and run through the creek to the other side. "Simonton," I yell again in desperation, bending at my waist to catch my breath. I've been in these parts many times before, but on this night, the weather makes it impossible for me to know my whereabouts. I continue moving through the woods, holding the lantern high, and using my forearm as a shield to keep the rain from crashing onto my face.

After pushing a few miles into the woods, I call out Simonton's name every so often. The muscles in my legs burn, and there is sharp pain in both feet. Out of nowhere, a squealing growl comes from nearby. I've heard the sound before and know it can only come from a wild boar.

I turn in the direction of the growl. My eyes widen and my chin quivers. The growl gets louder. I turn and scurry over the damp terrain. My boots pushed deeply into the mud with every step, and I yank my feet up hard to keep a quick and steady pace. As I come to a short elevation, I lunge forward to clear a narrow stretch of fallen tree branches but slip on my way down. The lantern flies out of my hand, and I push both hands out to brace the fall. Water splashes on my face.

I lay on my side and reach for my knee. "Awe," I whimper. I smack the ground with a clenched fist. "Damn." With both hands, I push up and pick up the lantern. The rain continues to crash down. I limp on for several hundred yards until I come to a small house buried deep into the woods. I'm not sure how far I have come, but I know I'm far away from home.

I creep to the side window and peek through. There are curtains hanging, but I don't see signs of light or fire burning on the inside of the house. I tiptoe to the front of the house and stand in front of the door. I'm relieved that the rain is no longer pounding the top of my head. The oak door has splintered in various sections, but it is sealed tightly around the edges. I take a deep breath before reaching for the doorknob. It doesn't budge. I go to the side of the house, pick up a large stone, and smash the window. I use the stone's edge to clear the glass debris on the lower part of the window, then stretch my arm through the opening and set the lantern on the floor. I grip the interior of the window and hoist myself up and pull my body through.

The wind whistles through the window. I hold the lantern high and notice that there are empty crates on the opposite wall. I stack the crates in front of the window to block the wind from coming through.

Fear settles in my stomach. I hold the lantern up and inspect the room. There are stacks of jars from from floor to ceiling covering two walls, and they are filled with a clear liquid. I pick up one of the bottles and twist the top, then angle my nose toward the opening. *Alcohol?* I jerk my head back quickly, squinting and wondering why there are so many jars of alcohol stacked in the house. *Moonshine?*

On the same wall as the window, I see small jars of preserves and a large bag of dry corn. My stomach growls. I reach into the corn sack, grab a handful of kernels, and push them into my mouth. I bite down hard on the corn, and it crumbles into pieces in my mouth. Since I had not eaten in several hours, the hard corn isn't bad at all. I open a bottle of the peach preserves, dip my fingers into the jar, and slurp the fruit into my mouth. I tilt my head back and dip my eyelids, enjoying the sweetness, then dig in with four fingers and pull out a bigger chunk this time. The sugary juice runs down my arm, and I lick it off.

After chowing on the kernels and preserves, I move the top crate to the side and peek my head through the opening. The harsh rain continues to hammer the earth. I am still for a moment. *Where's Simonton?* I dip my chin and move the crate back over the opening, then find a stack of gunny sacks and make a pillow and use the white sheets hanging on the back wall for covering. Before falling asleep, I sit with my back pressed firmly against the wall. A tear drops from my eyes, and I let it fall down my face. I settle into the sacks, and moments later, I doze off.

CHAPTER EIGHTEEN

I wake to a rattling truck engine. I get up from a sleeping position and gasp for air. "Oh shoot," I blurt, startled that I'm in an unusual place. Light peeks around the edges of the crates and seeps into the room. I also see light coming through various seams in the structure. Hanging on the back wall are long, white sheets and hoods, and I recognize the embossed white cross emblem outlined in red. *What in Heavens*... the engine gets closer. It is coming from the opposite side of the broken window. I spring from the floor and charge my way to the window. When I realize I don't have the lantern, I run back and grab it. But before I can lift myself to the window, I hear truck doors slam and two men talking. The voice of one of the men sounds like Furly.

"So, all we gotsta do is keep moving these things throughout the county. Ain't nobody gon' stop it. And hell, if the people want it, what's so bad 'bout giving it to 'em?"

The men laugh. "You got ya self a point there. But you know we can't just give it away though. We make it exclusive, not so easy to get." Furly lets off a boisterous laugh.

Several footsteps stomp onto the porch.

My heart beats fast. I lift myself, move through the window opening, and dart into the woods to find the widest tree trunk to hide behind. I peek one eye out from behind the trunk. Just before sliding the key into the lock, the man stops, pulls the key back, and reaches toward his waist. He turns in the direction of the brush leading into the wood, then whispers something to Furly.

Both men step off the porch and move slowly to the side of the house. The man pulls a gun from his waist and gazes in my direction. As they pass the width of the house, Furly sees the broken window, turns to the other man and they nod to each other. Furly then pulls his gun from the small of his back.

"Somebody out there. And when we find out who you are, you gon' be dealt with." Furly says, in a mean tone. He pulls the hammer back on the revolver. "So, you might as well come on out now, so we can try to work this thing out befo' it gets serious."

I tremble, interlock my fingers and pray. Sweat drips down my face. I turn and go deeper into the woods. When I glance back, I see them running in my direction. I jump over several small patches of murky slush and slip through narrow openings between the tree trunks. I whip my head around and see Furly raise his gun and point it directly at me. I reach the end of a flat stretch and leap down the steep decline. *Pow.* A shot rings out, the echo flares by my ears, and the bullet snaps through the tree branches. I pump my arms and legs faster, and I go deeper into the woods.

When I make it through a good part of the lowland, I hear Simonton's infamous bark. I follow the sound, and when I cross into the edge of a cemetery, I hear him ripping through the shrubs in my direction. Simonton is soaked, and he pants uncontrollably. He jumps on me. "Where you been boy?" I say, cheerfully. "You gon' get us in trouble."

It takes another hour for me and Simonton to make it back home. The sky is gray and thick puffy clouds linger over the house. Puffs of smoke emanate from the chimney. I lock Simonton into the stall next to Thunder and scold him. "Boy, you better start listening to me when I call you. You gon' get us killed one of these days. You hear me?" Simonton drops his head in shame.

"Sol," Mama yells from the opened door.

"Ma'am."

"Come on in here. It's cold out there."

As soon as I step into the house, Mama grabs my shoulders and pulls me in tightly. "Where you been son?"

I take a deep breath. "Simonton got on a hot trail and couldn't stop."

"It's been storming all night though, Sol. You can't be out there in no storm like that. You'll catch pneumonia and die. Look at you. You dripping wet. Now, get in there and change up into some warm clothes. I'll get you some grits going and some warm milk."

Mama heats up a big pale of water and gives it to me. I soap my body up real good and sprinkle the warm water over my head. After drying up, I put on some warm sleeping clothes and snuggle under the blankets.

I think about the entire night and wonder if those men would really kill me. I'm suprised to know Furly might be in the Klan. *I hope I'm not the next one hanging from the Old Oak.*

SOL & SIMONTON

CHAPTER NINETEEN

Mama didn't ask any more questions about being out in the woods all night, so I didn't offer. *Tell her I got shot at? Nope.* I have to train Simonton harder in order to get him to comply. I've had enough of him running off into the woods and know it will eventually lead to his death, or maybe even my own death. I carry a folded newspaper at all times and push it deeply into my back pocket and use it whenever Simonton doesn't act right. I also have a clicker to send a unique sound to Simonton to let him know when he's doing good.

To get Simonton used to the scent of coons, I make a trap out of chicken wire and put it just at the base of the woods with chopped up pieces of a bluegill I caught at the creek. Two days later, I trap a feisty coon that yelps and claws as soon as he sees me get close. I loop a rope through the holes in the chicken wire and pull the makeshift trap across the yard and throw it into the back of the wagon. I hook Thunder up to the wagon and move along the road at a steady pace. When I get to Willie's yard, his dogs circle the wagon and let off deep howling barks.

"Hey." Willie's voice drags longer than needed.

I jump from the wagon's seat. "Hey cut'n Willie."

"Hey, Sol. What bring you down that road, young man?"

"I caught a coon, and I want you to help me skin 'im."

"What?" Willie raises up from the chair. "Y'all den got a coon already?"

I point at the cage. "I trapped this one here. Tryna use 'im to train Simonton on how to find that coon scent."

"Oh, okay. Where ol' Simonton anyway?"

"I left him at home, locked him up. He been running in the woods after everything. Just about to get hisself killed out there."

"So, whatchu tryna do?"

"I reckon you'a show me how to skin a coon. I'll use the skin to train him on how to trail coon scent and not be out there chasing squirrels and rabbits and all that other stuff."

Willie moves to the back of the wagon and pulls the cover back. The coon growls. "Whoa cut'n. You gotta big one here. He probably ova fifteen pounds. That there is good eating."

"Where should I put Thunder?"

Willie points. "Put him ova there near that well. It's plenty of shade and water ova there. You can close that gate and let him have a good ole time in there."

"Okay."

I unhitch Thunder and walk him to the enclosed area. Willie picks the trap up from the back of the wagon and drags it to a covered area. He then lifts it on top of a huge wooden table. The coon growls and claws at Willie. "This one here gon' fight 'til the end." Willie takes a metal pipe and tilts his head to eye the opening of the pipe. He pushes thick rope through the hole in the center of the pipe with his thumb and index finger and the rope exits the other end. He then pushes the pipe through one of the hexagonal openings in the chicken wire. I watch his every move. He pokes at the coon with the pipe and the coon swipes and snarls. Willie eventually gets the rope around the coon's neck and he grips the rope hanging from the pipe on his side and pulls. The coon flips onto his back and begins to claw away at the air with each strike losing intensity and eventually coming to a stop.

"That's about it there. He gone now," Willie says. "Now, go over there and get me that bucket in the shed. I sprint to the shed and retrieve the bucket full of sharp objects and tools.

Willie shows me each step to skin a coon. While he cuts and pulls the skin away from the coon's flesh, he closes one eye. I stand back and fight to block the images of blood out of my mind.

"Don't be afraid. Comere." I inch closer to Willie. The coon lies flat on the table with blood splattered and pooled around his body. "Touch this fur here. Same thing my daddy showed me when I was a boy."

I feel tension in my body and my arms shake. I stretch my hand forward, and I see my hand tremble. "It's all right," Willie assures me. My hand stops just before I touch the coon. "C'mon cut'n." I touch the fur. The tips prickle my hand initially, but when I push deeper into the fur, it gets softer and feels smooth between my fingers. My anxiety subsides.

"It won't take you long to get over it." Willie mumbles through his teeth. "I was the same way as a boy. Couldn't stand to see no blood. My daddy use to take me out there in them woods and tell me to roam free, 'cause that's the only place a black man really feel free, you know? Cain't nobody tell you which way to go, especially witcha coonhound and you on your own land. He'a take you where them coons is—that's what he suppose to do. But you," Willie points directly at my chest, "you gotta know where you going. You cain't give white folks no reason to question you 'bout nothin'."

I tilt my head and shift my gaze away from Willie. "I lost my first puppy when I was six years old. It wasn't even my fault. He just ran out on that road and a truck hit 'im. And they neva' turned around or nothin'. I didn't even get a chance to ever train 'im. My mama told me I'd get another pet again." I shake my head; tears fill my eyes.

Willie takes a deep breath. "That happens in life. You can't let that getchu down. You gotta hound dog now, and we gon' turn him into a good one."

"I want him to be the best in the county. I figure we teach him to stop running in the woods like that and he gon' be a good one."

"It's gon' take a lot to turn him into the best in the county now," Willie chuckles.

I turn to Willie. "I'm ready to work." Willie shows me every single detail of the coon's anatomy. He then packages the skin into a brown paper bag and tosses it to me. "So, make sure you use small pieces of the fur. Some of that is real good fur. Heck, you can keep some of it and make yo' mama some slippers for when it get real cold. She'a like that. I'ma take this meat here and put it in the freezer. Next time you come down here, getcho meat and a few sweet potatoes and you got ya self one of the best meals ever—um um um."

"So, how do I get Simonton to trail coons with this?"

"Oh, okay. You get ya self a string and tie a small piece of that fur to the end of it. Start in the yard—just in the yard. Pull the string across the yard and start moving it around in patterns. You understand?"

I nod. "Yessir."

"That scent gon' be getting on the grass. Then, you take yo' dog and put him on the start of the pattern—that's ya trail. Now, when he get on it, you clap and cheer him on."

"What about a clicker?"

"You den got ya self a clicker?" I smile. "Yeah. You can use the clicker too. But the most important thing is that you congratulate him when he hit that trail. You use that clicker and give him a little piece of bacon or a treat."

"So, that's it?"

"Well, if you don't want him chasing rabbits or squirrels you do just the opposite. You run they skin on the ground and whack 'im when he get on they trail. That way, he'a know...never get on that trail."

I learned a lot from Willie, and I'm eager to get back home to try some new things with Simonton. Before I leave, Willie tosses me a pocketknife.

"You gon' need one of these when you out there in them woods. You neva know whatchu gon' come across. If you get too many coons on a hunt, you might have to skin 'em right out there in them woods to shift the weight. And when you get probably fifteen or something like that, you gon' need ya own shotgun." My ears are wide open. "Get 'im on up here by the end of spring and we'a put 'im out there wit' ol Redbone and Bluetick and let them run out there in them woods. But right now, you just keep 'im 'round the house, don't go too far up in the woods, let him learn some stuff first."

I smile. "Thank you, cut'n Willie." I'm ready to train him now.

CHAPTER TWENTY

The sun is up and shining brightly when I arrive home. I see Pastor Williams's truck slanted across the yard. I cut across the back of the property and put Thunder in his stall. Since Mama hasn't been sharing much with me, I know she must be telling the Pastor everything about her being in jail. I sneak to the side of the house and place my ear close to the wall to hear the conversation. I don't want her to get into any more trouble with the law.

I move my head up slowly and peek over the bottom of the window frame to see Pastor Williams leaning with his back firmly against the chair. Mama sits opposite of him with her elbow on the table and her forehead buried into the palm of her hand while she looks at a crumpled piece of white paper with a long horizontal crease that makes the top of the paper flare up.

"Now Kat, lemme check into it. Ain't like you the only ones 'round here that got one of them notices. They prolly went all up and down that road out there and got all the black people they could and put these notices on they houses," Pastor Williams says, almost pleading and motioning with his hands.

Mama's eye gloss as she tries to hold back tears. "That ain't what that letter sayin' pastor—you know that. They say they gon' take the property cause I ain't fix that fence out there—some type of lien...and if I don't pay 'em that money they gon' take this farm that's been in my family since slavery ended—and ain't nobody taking nothin' from me. Ain't nobody got that type of money just laying 'round here. Where am I gon' come up with forty seven dollars from?" Her voice carries the painful sorrow that I've often heard when women cry. It crackles, and she swallows in mid-sentence trying to contain her emotion.

Pastor Williams reaches for her flaccid hand and cups it into his hands. "Listen. You ain't gettin' no shotgun, no knife, no skillet—nothin, you hear me?" Mama chuckles. Pastor grins and grips her hand tighter. "For real, Kat. Ain't nobody playin' witchu. We gon' pray that God intervene like he always do and make everything just right. That's the only way we can do it."

Mama turns her shoulders begrudgingly, then gives him a nod with her lips pressed together tightly. Mama tells him she has ninety days to pay or our land is gone. My arms get heavy, my shoulders slump, and I feel rage inside of me like boiling water in a hot pot. I move away from the window with my head buried in my chest. The porch squeaks with each step that Mama and Pastor Williams take. I tiptoe behind the truck, pretending that I just made it home. When Mama sees me, her head tilts up and she presses her lips back.

Pastor Williams' eyes follow her gaze. "Hello, Sol," Pastor Williams says, stepping off the porch. "How you doing, son?"

I smile and give him a quick nod. "I'm fine, sir."

Pastor Williams opens his mouth wide and his teeth look like even sections of a railroad track. "I hear you training ya dog," Pastor Williams says, still showing his teeth. "He gon' be a good one or what?"

"Yessir. He gon' be a good one."

"He'a coonhound?"

"Yessir."

"All right, nah. I betta see some furs and some slippers 'round here. And I want some of that good ole meat. People pay a lot for that stuff 'round here."

"Yessir." I say, under my breath, and I feel a burst of delight swelling in my chest.

"The Lord is good."

"Hallelujah," Mama responds.

Pastor Williams steps off the porch where the glare of the sun hits him, and he shields his eyes with his hand like a saluting officer. "Don't forget what I said, Kat. It shall all come to pass; just a little faith is enough. Our God is not asking for much." He finally drops his hand. "Just a little faith," Pastor reiterates. "God bless you and give you more strength."

Mama clasps her hands in front of her and nods. "Amen, Pastor. Thank you very much."

When Pastor Williams turns, he smiles at me on the way to his truck. "Whatchu wanna be when you grow up, son?" he asks.

I look at Mama and she smiles and gives me a subtle nod. I clear my throat and answer, "I wanna to be a pilot in the Navy, sir."

Pastor Williams tips his hat. "You've got ya'self a fine young man, Kat," he says. "And I pray God will grant your heart's desire."

Mama and I say, "Amen" and Pastor Williams stretches his right hand toward me for a handshake. I take the handshake quickly, and Pastor closes his left hand on our grip. "God bless you, son. You've got to be strong for your mama. You hear me?"

I nod slowly. "Yessir."

"Bye now," Pastor Williams says, and walks to his truck and opens the whining truck door.

Mama and I walk back into the house. Mama makes me a sandwich, and I chow it down. My eyes are heavy so I lower my head between my folded arms and doze off.

I wake to Mama sitting next to me. She closes her eyes tight, places her palm on my shoulder, and begins to pray. When she's done praying, I open my eyes. "Amen," she says. "We'll talk in the morning," she whispers. "I gotta go deliver a baby out near the Ridge tonight. I should be back in the mo'nin. Get ya self up and go to ya room and get some rest."

"Yes ma'am." I retreat to my room and bury myself into the warm covers. I hear Mama in her room preparing her medical bag. *Pastor said people pay good money for furs and coon meat, and I need to help my mama and save our farm. I'm gon' get Simonton out there in a few nights to get us some coons.* I lift myself from the bed and light the candle on the desk. I peel back the cover of the Bible and read from the book of Psalms, Chapter 91. When I finish, I close the Bible and blow out the flame from the candle.

A horn blares from the outside and I hear Mama grabbing her bag. "See you later, son. Sleep tight, and make sure you get up early and tend to your chores," she yells from the other room.

"Yes ma'am."

Two crickets chirp one after the other as if in tune. A light wind whistles outside the window and a cold chill runs up my spine. I lower myself into the bed and wrap the covers up to my chin, and stare into the ceiling. "Please, dear Lord, bless my mother and don't allow our house to be taken away," I whisper to myself. *Me and Simonton gon' make a lot of money catching coons.*

* * *

I toss and turn throughout the night and can't seem to fall into a deep sleep. I am awakened by Simonton's loud howl. I rise from the bed and peer through the window. The sky is dark and full of sparkling stars. Simonton howls again, this time louder, and then one after another. I slip on my boots, push my arms into a heavy coat, and pull a cap down on my head.

It's time to catch some coons.

I slip the knife into one of the coat's pockets and button the flap, then I pour some oil into the lantern and strike a match to light the wick. I stand in the doorway and glance back at Mama's room. I walk back into the house and get the shotgun from behind Mama's door.

I step off the front porch. The cool wind hits my face and my nose twinkles. It's much too cold out here, so I sit the lantern on the porch and reach into my coat pocket for gloves and slip my fingers into them. I take long strides across the yard with the lantern held steady in front of me. When Simonton sees me come through the barn door, he howls louder and scratches the stall door with his front paws. I open the door, and Simonton shoots by me and dashes toward the woods.

"Hold boy, sit," I command, stomping my foot to emphasize my point. Simonton turns, darts back to me, and sits next to my foot. "Good boy. Good boy." I reach into my coat pocket, pull out a small chunk of bacon and hold it above Simonton's mouth, then I drop it. Simonton snatches it before it hits the ground and gobbles it down.

My heart pounds hard and fast like a drum is planted in my chest. My throat tightens, and I realized this is the moment I had been waiting for.

Simonton is eager. He sits anxiously and whines, clawing at the gravel with his two front paws, waiting for me to give him the command. He jerks forward like a sprinter anticipating the blast from a starting gun.

"Scat now!" I order. Simonton shoots out like a missile. He hits the entry of the woods fast, and I'm in full stride doing my best to tail him. I try to keep the lantern steady, but the light flickers around on the thicket of the woods with each stride I take on the bumpy ground. *This is it.* His deep howl is like music to my ears. "Get 'im boy!" I yell. My chest pumps in and out, and I stop and bend at my waist to catch my breath. His bark becomes fainter as he drifts deeper into the woods. I tilt my head up and look into the sky.

The trees tower over me and the sound of chirping crickets is intense. Simonton's howls become more consistent. *His first coon.* I feel butterflies in my stomach as I move through the brush in the direction of the barks. When I get close, I see Simonton's front legs fully engaged with the trunk of a tree making me grin from ear to ear. "Get 'im boy," I scream. "Good boy. You did good." From my pocket, I pull out another piece of bacon and offer it to Simonton. This time, he is too focused on the coon to accept it. He howls louder. I lean the shotgun against a tree then extend the lantern high above my head to see if I can see the coon's beady eyes. "There he is!" I shout. I move to the other side of the tree to get a better view. Simonton shifts with me and stays fixated on the coon. I marvel in the moment. I sit and watch my dog howl for several more minutes before deciding to move on. "It's okay buddy. You did your job."

I pull on Simonton's collar to convince him to leave the tree. With a few whacks of the folded newspaper, Simonton finally complies. When we get several feet from the tree, we hear a fumbling in the trees and a muffled thud sound. Simonton turns and jets in the direction of the tree. His howl quickly turns into a growl. I panic and run after him. "Simonton!" I yell.

I run into a steep decline that drops off sharply. I lose my balance for a moment but regain it and continue to follow Simonton's bark. Simonton's bark gets louder, and I know I am closer to him. His growls are fierce. When I steady the lantern to face level, I see Simonton faced off with a coon. The coon backs up against a tree and snarls, while showing his teeth. Simonton growls, then charges directly at the coon. I raise the shotgun and aim.

"Hold boy!" I yell, but it's too late. Simonton tangles with the coon and the two claw and snap at each other for a good amount of time. Simonton finally catches him by the neck and swings him against the ground several times until his body goes limp. The coon's lower body lies peacefully on the dirt, while Simonton's jaws are still locked on his neck. *He's dead.*

I stand with my mouth wide open, holding the lantern in one hand and the shotgun in the other. "Come here boy," I whisper. I kneel and Simonton moves between my legs. "Good boy. You did good." I rub the top of his head. The coon lies with blood dripping out the side of his mouth.

I grip the coon by the fur on his back and drop him into a

gunny sack, then fling the sack over my shoulder. My chest is full of pride. I get excited about the many journeys Simonton and I will go on. He tries to run other trails, but I command him to stay and he complies.

When we arrive home, I lock Simonton in the small stall. I give him more treats and congratulate him on treeing his first coon. "You did good boy. I'm so proud of you." *I can't wait to tell Willie about it.* It is past midnight when we make it back to the house. Mama is still out delivering a baby and has not returned home yet. I wipe the shotgun down good and put it behind Mama's door. I use the knife Willie gave me to skin and clean the coon just like he showed me. I don't want to leave Simonton out, so I light a fire on the stove and boil a piece of the coon meat just for him. When the meat is done, I take it to the barn and share it with Simonton. He chows down on it and smacks his mouth as if to ask for more.

I know Mama will ask questions about the coon meat in the ice box so I push it to the back and hope she doesn't see it when she comes home. I clean up the kitchen area and leave the fur in the barn to clean in the morning. As I lay in bed, I smile thinking about Simonton and his first showing in the woods. *Simonton treed his first coon in only a few minutes. I got myself a great coonhound.* I adjust my pillow, close my eyes, and fall asleep.

CHAPTER TWENTY-ONE

The next morning...

The sun hides behind a thick, gray cloud, and with it comes a cold breeze. I'm chopping firewood, and I see a blue truck veer off the main road and pull into the driving path leading to the house. Mama must've caught a glimpse of the truck through the window or heard the tires cutting through the rocks embedded in the red dirt. There are two men in the truck and Movery's father is the only person I know with a truck that looks like that.

Mama moves gingerly through the doorway onto the porch and eases herself into the chair, never letting her eyes off the truck. She lifts her chin and pans her head with the movement of the truck until it comes to a stop.

Simonton howls and trots to the truck. "Hold boy." I command him. Simonton stops his charge but continues to howl from just the place where I gave the command. The engine quiets, both truck doors swing open and a loud squeaking sound comes with it.

Movery's dad is short and stocky. He's wearing a soiled cap and a thick tan coat. The other man is tall and medium built. His steps are slow and he walks with a slight spring from his heels. He takes a few steps and leans against the truck, fires up a cigarette, and gazes into the woods. Movery steps out of the driver's side after her father. Her eyes are damp and she's biting her bottom lip.

"Mo'nin, Miss Katherine," Movery's dad says, taking his hat off just long enough for the greeting and continuing to the porch. Movery lingers behind him, stops halfway to the porch, and moves towards me. When our eyes meet she drops her chin into her chest, turns slightly away from me, and tries to hold back tears, but can't. I wrap my arm around her shoulder and pulled her close to me.

"Mo'nin, Kenneth. How you doing this mo'nin?" Mama says.

Kenneth sighs. "Just coming through here to see if y'all might'a seen my son, Kenneth Junior. Ain't nobody seen him since yesterday and that ain't like 'im. Last time we saw 'im he was going to town to pick up a few things fo' his mama, and ain't came back." Kenneth is Movery's older brother and he's seventeen years old.

"My God," Mama says, with a grimace, "ain't nobody heard from 'im?"

Kenneth shakes his head slowly. "No. Nothing. That's why I'm going around town tryna find out where he might be. I know he been to that juke joint, and I scolded him for that. But he ain't one to be gone all night like this. That just ain't my boy."

"My God," Mama says again, shaking her head.

Kenneth takes a long breath. "Cain't go to the sheriff."

"You ain't neva lied," Mama says.

"They don't bit mo' care 'bout no black folk much as they care for a squirrel or a old hog or somethin'."

"Now, me and Sol can get our old horse and get out there and help y'all if you want. Won't be no problem at all."

Movery tilts her head up and looks me in the eyes. "I want my brother," she says, then buries her forehead into my chest. I hold her tighter.

"He gon' be all right," I whisper.

I know deep down in my heart that a black boy is no different from hunting animals out there in the woods. As much as I want to tell Movery the truth about what I feel in my gut, I know I have to say nice things to keep her from thinking the worst.

"Ain't no need just yet, Miss Katherine," Kenneth says. "We gon' get on up the road and go down yonder. Just get the word out if you hear something or see somebody, okay?"

"I sure will. And we'a be praying."

"You have a good day now," Kenneth says.

The dark man turns and opens the passenger side door on the truck. Kenneth moves toward the truck, while Movery drifts back to the truck at a snail's pace.

Mama stands from the chair. "Kenneth. Why don't you have your girl stay here while y'all do ya searching." She gestures to him. "She'a be okay here. She don't need to be going with y'all. She'a be safe right here. That child just as scared about her brother and don't need to be out there with y'all."

Kenneth ponders. "Mo', you okay here?" By this time, Mama makes her way to Movery and wraps her arm around the top of her back and rests her palm on the opposite shoulder.

Movery nods. "Yes. I'a stay here."

"Okay. I'll come back later to getchu." The men get back into the truck, fire up the engine, and pull away.

Mama spends time showing Movery how to bake cookies and knit. Movery's smile brightens every time Mama shows her something new. I go to the yard and to train Simonton. I tie a piece of the raccoon's fur to a long string and create trails for Simonton to follow. Each time he follows the trail, I give him a treat and rub his head. I can't stop thinking about what might have happened to Junior. I want to help, but I don't know what to do. *Maybe Kenneth Junior just decided to leave after his daddy whooped him something good after the last time he went to the juke joint.* I lock Simonton into the small stall next to Thunder and close the barn. When I make it back to the house, I smell the aroma of fresh baked cookies. Mama and Movery had stacked the cookies on a plate, and they are still knitting.

Movery looks on as Mama instructs her from her chair. "See, all you have to do is take this through here and pull. When you have this row done, you start on the next one and just keep going 'til you finish."

"Hey, Sol," Movery says, "your mama the best. She showed me how to bake cookies, and now I'm knitting. I even told her that I'm the one who gave you the magazine."

I raise my eyebrows just as Mama smirks. "Yeah. He been telling me he bought the thing from the store..."

"But-but..."

"It's okay, boy," Mama says, "I knew you was lying when ya eyes started moving all around in ya head." Movery and Mama laugh.

"Won't y'all get ya self some cookies and milk? I gotta go out here and get the clothes off the line. I'a be right back." She picks up a basket and walks out the door.

I take a deep breath and sit at the table, opposite of Movery. "So, whatchu thinking?"

Movery chews on a cookie and shakes her head. "I dunno. Junior ain't neva left like this. I just hope ain't nobody got 'im and planning on beatin' him or hanging him or nothin' like that."

"Did he say anything?"

"The only thing I can think of...is he told me a man in town approached him last week and asked if he the one who broke into the house. Junior ain't even know the man, but he just came up asking him about some house and if he broke into it."

My face goes blank and my heart drops to the bottom of my stomach. "Was it a white man?"

"Yeah. He didn't really describe him. Just said he was white and just came up to him asking that. Now, Junior ain't neva stole nothing or broke into nobody house or nothing. Even when he went to the juke joint, he told my daddy the truth."

I place my forehead into the palm of my hands. "Oh no!" I grunt.

"What?"

"You said the white man asked if he broke into a house?"

Movery hesitates. "Yeah. He said something about breaking into a house."

I clench my fists and throw one into the air. "Damn!"

"What's wrong?" Movery eyes are bulging. "You know something about this? You know where Junior is?"

"Why does something always..."

Movery cuts me off. "What is it Sol?"

"These men..." I start, but I feel my hands shaking and my heart beating out of control. "One night, Simonton got out and I couldn't find him. I mean he went deep out there in them woods. I came across a small shack, and I broke into it because it was storming—I mean, the rain was pounding and pounding, and I got lost and didn't even know where I was. Inside, there wasn't nothing but bottles of moonshine or something and robes that they say the Klan wear."

Movery slumps into the back of the chair. "Oh my God."

"The next mornin', I wake up 'cause I hear somebody coming, so I jump through the window and ran to the woods. They heard me…"

"What happened next?" she says, with her eyebrows fully furrowed.

"Well, one of the men musta saw me from the back 'cause he shot at me."

"He shot at you?" she yells.

I reach forward and press one of my palms against her mouth. "Shhh. My mama gon' hear."

"Sol, y'all okay in there?" Mama's voice blasts like a screaming trumpet.

"We okay, Mama," I yell back.

Movery's hands tremble and she sits with her arms folded, and her eyes staring into nothingness. After a few seconds of intense processing, she says, "Let's go find the place."

"Go find it?" I ask.

"Yeah. We can't just have my brother out there and let these white folks kill 'im."

Mama steps back onto the porch and enters the house with the basket on her hip. "I thought y'all would have eaten up all the cookies by now."

"No ma'am. We just talkin'. But we finsta get us some milk and start eating some now." *Mama's not buying it*. She drops the basket from her hip, and it lands on the floor.

Before she could say anything, I start, "Mama can me and Movery go down to the creek?"

Mama pauses and scans the two of us with her eyes. "Y'all betta not go far. And come right back."

We make it to the creek and sit on the rock that we sit on every time we go there. Simonton moves around trees and goes to the creek and drinks. "Come here boy," I command him. He runs to me and starts sniffing around my feet. I rub his head. "Good boy. Good boy." Movery and I devise a plan to find the secret house that I came across in the woods. I tell her that Furly was one of the men, and I didn't recognize the other. Since I don't know exactly where the house is, we will need much of the day to find it. We agree to look for the house tomorrow if Junior doesn't return home by the morning.

"Should I tell my daddy about this?" Movery asks.

"I don't think you should, not now. We gotta find the house first. After we find it, then we can tell 'em where it is. The house might not have nothing to do with Junior. And what if they stop looking for him and go on what we say, and they miss him somewhere else?"

"You got a point," Movery concurs.

"So, let's meet here at the creek 'round seven in the morning. Tonight, I'll think about where I was when the big storm came and try to figure out how I got to the house."

When we return home, Mama is sitting on the porch sipping on tea. "Y'all have a good walk?

"Yes, ma'am," we chorus.

"Glad y'all came back befo' the sun drop. Look like it's gon' be cool tonight."

Mama lights a fire, and we all sit in the living room. Movery reads through some of the pages of Native Son while I thumb through the magazine.

Darkness begins to fill the house, and Mama lights a few candles. Moments later, a truck engine rattles, and I look out of the window. "I think that's yo' daddy, Mo." Movery stands from the chair and looks on with anticipation. I open the door and Kenneth makes his way to the steps.

"Come on in," Mama says.

Kenneth's feet appear heavy; he drags himself in. "Ain't had no luck. We been as far as Atmo' and nobody seen 'im."

Mama drops her head, then she picks it up quickly. "Well, let's stay hopeful. The Lord will see that he come home safe."

Kenneth's eyes blink and he nods slightly. "Let's see," Kenneth sighs, then shifts his eyes to Movery. "Let's go baby girl so you can get some sleep." Kenneth then turns to Mama. "Thank you, Miss Katherine."

"Any time, Kenneth. Yo baby is welcome here."

I turn in early. I want all the energy I can get so that we can find that house in the morning. I pack some cookies and stuff them into my coat pocket and get two containers and fill them with water. I get on my knees and pray for God's safety. I ask God to protect me and Movery. It hurts to see her cry, and I want to see her smile again.

CHAPTER TWENTY-TWO

"Good morning," I greet Mama and rub my eyes with the back of my hands. I have to get ready to meet Movery at the creek and go looking for Junior.

"Good morning," she murmurs, "sit down, Solomon." She pulls the chair back for me. "I gotta tell you something."

I know it's serious because she said my whole name. "Ma'am." My stomach rolls and I ease down in the chair.

She shifts her chair until she is directly facing me, and she sighs before she begins. "Son," she starts, "I want you to be safe out there." I stare at her and my face must show nothing but a stolid expression. She closes her hands together and places them on her knees. "You understand me? This whole thing about Junior being missing is scary. You gotta be careful. Watch where you go. Watch who you talk to, you hear me?"

"Yes, ma'am."

She looks squarely into my eyes. "I don't want nothing to happen to you."

I blink in quick successions. "Ain't nothin' gon' happen to me, mama."

"I can't be there for you all the time. You becoming a man, Sol." My stomach flutters. Mama's emotion is scaring me. After a long silence, she stands from the chair and moves to the stove. "I made you some grits and a few biscuits." She scoops a heap of grits into a bowl and sets it in front of me. "Go on in there and wash ya face and have some breakfast."

"Yes, ma'am." I stand and go to the sink to wash my face.

"Make sure you get them chickens fed befo' to do anything else today." Mama moves plates and bowls around on the table.

"Yes, ma'am."

A brief silence is broken when Mama says, "That Movery is a sweet girl." Her back is to me and I feel a quivering of my hands. I am still washing my face and not sure how much I should offer.

"We just friends mama." That's the best thing I come up with.

"Oh. I know that. Y'all way too young to be courtin'." Mama snaps her head at an angle. "Y'all just be friends, go to church, and school—that's it."

I smirk. "Ain't nobody thinking about courtin' no girls yet mama."

Mama smiles back. "You bet not. 'Cause you know I'a kill you if you come up here talkin' 'bout you gotta a baby comin'."

I cover my face with one of my hands. "Oh my God."

"Don't be actin' like you don't know what I'm talkin' about, boy."

"Movery is my best friend. She's not my girlfriend," I plead, with a slight grin. I sit and take two deep plunges into the grits with a spoon. *While we're talking about Movery, I might as well tell her part of my plan today.* "Well, we going to the creek today."

"The creek?"

"Yeah. I'ma meet her down there this morning. She worried about Junior and we gon' talk. Might do a little fishing." I'm happy to get it off my chest. I'm proud I don't have to lie about meeting Movery.

Mama lifts her chin eyes and plants her eyes on me. "Okay. Y'all don't be out there late either. Get on back home, okay?"

"Yes, ma'am."

When I make it to the creek, it is strangely quiet except for the frogs croaking. I sit on the rock and wait for Movery. Mama knows I'm about to be a man. That makes me feel both proud and scared. I hope I can help find Junior and bring him back to his family. A turtle dives into the water and I hear the splashing water. I pick up a rock and start to fling it at the turtle's head. I hold the rock in the air for a moment, then sling it into the woods. Moments later, I hear footsteps snapping brittle branches. I jerk my head in the direction of the sound and see Movery. She wearing a coat, her arms folded and she's walking briskly through the vertical maze of tree trunks.

"Good mo'nin," I whisper.

"Hey Sol." We hug. "He still didn't come home." Movery's eyes are red and puffy. "So, what we gon' do?"

I ponder. "We gon' find that house and see what's going on. If that's the house the man was talking about, then all we have to do is find it and then come back and tell yo' daddy where it is. Then maybe he can question the men."

Movery shifts her shoulders and paces in a circle. "I don't know, Sol. This is all scary to me. I mean, my brother is gon' for like two days and nobody know where he is." Tears flow down Movery's face.

"Don't cry. Don't cry. Let's get going."

I guide Movery through the woods and mark trees using my pocket knife so that I can remember how to get back to the creek. I'm happy I didn't bring Simonton along, because he would run freely in the woods and might cause more trouble. After trekking through the woods for a couple of hours, we sit on a dead stump, eat cookies, and drink from the container I brought along with me.

Movery mutters. "You think we going in the right direction?"

I curl my bottom lip and look around. "I think we are...but some of these trees look the same."

"I think we should go back, Sol. We been out here too long, and it don't look like nothing out here."

I stand on a slight elevation and point. "Okay, I think we go through there. C'mon." I rush through the thicket of tree branches with Movery close behind. We push through a long stretch until we come to an opening. I turn to Movery and whisper. "That's it." I bend at the knees and move behind a thick tree trunk. There are two trucks parked near the house and a plume of smoke rising from the chimney.

"What they doing in there?" Movery asks.

"They probably doing all kinda stuff."

A white man exits the house and steps into one of the trucks, then drives off.

Movery turns to me. "Who is that? Have you ever seen him before?"

"No. I don't know who that is."

Movery sighs. "I think we should leave. We already marked the trees. We can go home and tell ma daddy to come here and see what they doing. They might know where Junior is."

I whip my finger in front of my mouth. "Shhh." Another man walks out of the house. He strikes a match and lights up a cigarette, then drifts down the driving path away from the house, holding the cigarette between his fingers and puffing out smoke like he's on a peaceful stroll.

"Wait right here. I'ma go see what they doing."

Movery grabs my wrist. "What? You not going over there. What den got into yo' crazy mind?"

"Look. I'ma go over there and look through the window. If I don't see nothing, then I'ma come back and we can leave."

"I don't like this." Movery's chin quivers.

"Just wait and I'a be right back."

I creep to the back of the house and tiptoe to the window. The window is boarded up, so I can't see anything inside. I bend and move to the other window, and it is also boarded up. I glance back at Movery. She hisses, and swings her hand toward her body sharply, signaling for me to *come back*.

I return a blank face and a *give me a second* gesture with my mouth without uttering a sound. *Lord, I hope there are only two men here.* I ease around to the front door. It is tightly sealed just as I had seen it before. I take a long breath before reaching my hand down to the brass knob. I turn the knob ever so slightly and it squeaks. I push the door open slowly. The rusty hinges screech as the space widens. Inside, I see Junior tied to a chair with his chin sunk deep into his chest. Junior raises his head slowly when he hears the door open. The door squeals, and I whip my head around. I feel the air rush and a *thud*. The door is shut. Junior's eyebrows are compressed, and he wobbles in the chair trying to break loose. I take quiet steps to Junior, who moves anxiously. His hands are tied with a thick rope. I pull out my pocketknife and cut the rope.

"How you find me?" Junior utters, panting and pulling the rope away from his wrists.

"Shhh," I put my finger in front of his mouth. We move slowly out of the house and sprint to where Movery waits. Junior's shirt is dirty and dangling around his neck, and he limps. Movery bubbles with joy when she sees Junior, but her joy quickly turns to fear when the man steps back onto the porch. As soon as we hit the edge of the woods, we turn and sprint as fast as we can without looking back. Junior gets tired about a quarter of a mile into the woods and we stop. He bends over to catch his breath.

"Y'all don't know how happy I was to see y'all." Junior says, gasping for air. Movery hugs him tightly. "They was gon' hang me tonight, Mo."

I'm still anxious. "We gotta keep running." I give Junior some water and he gulps it down.

"You right. Let's keep running," Junior says, while trying to control his breathing.

It is late in the afternoon when we make it to the creek. Junior explains to us that the men accused him of breaking into the house and stealing stuff. They saw him in town, snatched him, and threw him into the back of a truck. Several men beat him and for two days and they only gave him water.

We rush to Movery's house and when we get near the small barbed-wire fence separating the house from the pasture, Movery's father steps off the porch. "Daddy!" Junior yells. Kenneth freezes and turns in direction of Junior's voice. He drops a hand tool and runs to Junior. They hug tightly as Movery and I watch on.

Tears fill Kenneth's eyes. "What happened?"

Junior tries to tell him, but his voice crackles. "They was gon' hang me talking 'bout I stole something. I ain't did nothing, daddy. You know I don't be stealing from nobody."

Movery's mother bursts out the house and runs to Junior. "My baby." She is a heavy-set woman with short, gray hair. "Praise the Lord! Praise the Lord!"

"I love you mama," Junior whines.

Before they enter the house, Kenneth tells me he's going to take me to Willie's house since he lives right up the road, and Willie can take me home.

For the next hour, Junior sits at the dining table and shares the gruesome treatment he experienced over the previous two days. Movery and I sit on the porch, but she had propped the door open wide enough to hear. With every detail, his mother shrieks, and it pains me in my gut knowing the men were really looking for me. *I want to tell somebody, but I know this ain't the right time.*

Kenneth tells Junior to get cleaned up. "Now, y'all know where the shotgun is. I'ma take Sol up the road, and I'a be right back." Movery pulls the door shut, and we sit on the porch pretending to be having a conversation. The door opens. "C'mon here, son. Lemme take you to Willie's."

When we get to Willie's, he's sitting on the porch like he always is. He has no problem taking me home. "C'mon, let's go."

On the ride home, I share with Willie what happened the night Simonton got lost, and I ended up at the same place Junior was found. He doesn't say much; he mostly responds with, "Um-hmm" and "Uh-huh". I also share that the men must have mistaken Junior for me and would probably be looking for me too.

Willie breaks his silence. "I appreciate you telling me this, Sol. But for us, it really don't matter. They could've pulled any ole black boy off the road and kilt 'im. That's how they are. They'a hang you high from a tree just fo' looking at 'em wrong. But we ain't gon' let that happen no mo', trust me." Silence fills the air again. I had never heard a black man speak with so much courage before in my life.

The truck pulls into the yard. Mama is sitting in her chair. She raises her arm slightly and stands from her chair. "Hey there. Y'all find 'im?"

We get out of the truck. Willie smiles. "Yeah, he at home now."

"Praise God! Ain't God good?" I run to Mama and give her a big hug.

"Sol can explain everything to you. It's a long story. We'a be talkin' in the morning."

Mama squints. "Is everything okay?"

"Well, it's the same ole thang, but we'a handle it," Willie mumbles through his tight lips. "Aye, y'all got a shotgun in there?"

Mama's face twists. "Whatchu mean?"

"You gotta be ready," Willie insists.

"Yeah. I have one."

"Okay. I'ma go by Charlie's and tell him to come here in the mornin. Sol gon' have ta tell 'em where that place is."

Mama jerks her head from Willie to me, then back to Willie. "What place y'all talkin' 'bout?" I drop my head.

"He'a tell ya. I gotta get back home."

Mama's eyes are on Willie as he pulls himself into the truck. He yanks the truck into drive, and the truck pulls off. I stay up and tell Mama the whole story about chasing after Simonton and discovering the secret house during the storm. Mama's face is blank most of the time, and she stares into the floor whenever I share details about the ordeal. *Things will never be the same, and I don't wanna die.*

CHAPTER TWENTY-THREE

I sleep in longer than I expected. I unravel from the covers and gaze out of the window to see the sun casting a feeble glow. It wraps around the expanse of the tall hickory trees. I hear the rhythmic sounds of a sputtering truck engine, and I know what the visit is all about. Mama had sobbed all night and tried to keep quiet by burying her head deep into a pillow, but I heard the muffled prayers through the wall.

I keep seeing horrific images of Junior hanging from a tree. I had promised to take Kenneth to the exact location of the secret house, and every time I think about it, I feel a knot tighten in the bottom of my gut. My eyes move to the door of my mother's room, and I notice that the door is ajar. Mama never leaves her door open when she's in the house.

I walk to the front door. It's Charlie's truck, and he stops near the porch. Charlie opens the driver's side door and steps out. Seconds later, Mama opens the other door and exits. A cool breeze hits my face as I step onto the porch. Charlie and Mama move quickly into the house. "It's cold out there. You betta get some sleeves on ya," Mama says, as she passes me in the doorway.

Charlie pulls his hat off his head before entering the house. Once in, he turns to me. "Tell me what happened," he says, lifting his chin and maintaining a tight face.

I begin to recount the entire ordeal.

"I'll heat some tea while y'all talk," Mama interjects.

Charlie listens intently, and eventually takes a seat at the table. Every so often, he asks me to tell a particular detail over again. When I get to the part about Junior running and hugging Kenneth, Charlie takes a long sigh, sips from the teacup and stares me right in the eyes. "So, look..." he starts, "these white folk don't care nothin' 'bout us. You gotta know that. You going into that house is just enough for them to have you pulled from a truck and hanged from a tree. But we ain't gon' let that happen. That's not how we live in these parts. Ain't nobody running from them or nobody else. As soon as Kenny get on up here, we gon' take care of it."

Mama sits slowly, then taps her fingertips around the top teacup. "Charlie, y'all cain't let nothin' happen to my boy." Tears fill her eyes and she wipes them with her sleeve.

"Ain't nothin' gon' happened to him, sis. You know we gon' handle this. Ain't I always told you that?"

Mama nods her head. "Yeah. But we ain't tryna have them people after us. I told him to stay away from them folks, just get out they way. Him and that damn dog den got him in some trouble now and ain't nothin' we can do..." Mama shifts her shoulders to me. "Didn't I tell you not to be letting that dog run all over the place and go all up in them woods?"

"C'mon sis," Charlie pleads, and reaches for her shoulder. My chest pumps fast.

"Now, you den got ya self in trouble and them people might try ta kill you." I jerk away from the chair and dart into my room. I hear Charlie trying to plead with her.

"C'mon sis. The boy ain't did nothin'. He just went out in the woods."

"Oh. He ain't did nothin', Charlie?" Mama says. "He always want to do what he want to do. Them white folk don't care nothin' about him. They'a take his life and don't care two cents about it."

Charlie is quiet for a moment. "But sis, you know that ain't no way to live. Living in a cage ain't living. Living free is living. And you know me, ain't nothin' happening to you or that boy." I'ma wait outside fo' Kenny, then we gon' figure this here thing out. We'a be back later."

I look out the window and see Charlie taking a slow pace across the yard. I slip out the back door and walk to the barn. I see Charlie leaning against his truck.

"Where ya dog at?" he asks.

"He locked up in the barn," I say, while fiddling with a small stick.

"Aye, nephew. Ain't no reason to be hard on ya self. This hear ain't yo' fault. Sometime life just like that. But I need you to pick ya head up and listen to ya mama. I know she'a fireball, but she love you and ain't want nothin' but the best fo ya."

I raise my chin. "Yessir."

SOL & SIMONTON

Kenneth's truck pulls into the yard. Kenneth and Sho Boy spring out of the truck.

"Sho Boy," Charlie says, pressing one side of his mouth back into a grin. "What bring you back down to da'ville, boy?"

Sho Boy smirks and nods his head. "You know how things get, Cha'lie. Few thangs go wrong and you just get to the next spot."

Charlie chuckles. "The next spot, huh?" Sho Boy grins more. "Definitely good to see you though."

The three men exchange handshakes. "Damn glad to see you, boy," Charlie says.

"So, what we got?" Kenneth chimes in.

"Sol say the house down there near the end of the Washington Farm, on the edge, not far from where that cemetery used to be. Somewhere 'round that way it's some hills..."

Sho Boy squints. "Sound like ova there near that quarter-half that used to be owned by the Freeman family. You remember he and Bay Lee used to work fo' a white man back there in them woods doing metal?"

"Uh-huh," Charlie agrees.

"'Round 'bout where ole cut'n Joe used to own that little ten-acre piece."

"I know exactly where you talkin' 'bout."

Kenneth hawks and spit onto the ground. "Way, way back in them woods, huh?

"From what he say, that's 'round 'bout where is it."

I stand. "I marked the trees. When we got to the hilly parts," I point, "the house was about two miles going north."

Kenneth rubs his jaw. "How you know it's north?"

"'Cause the night I was out there following my dog, I kept

looking up at the big star, so I knew where I was going when I had to get back home."

Charlie nods his head. Kenneth concurs by dropping his hand from his jaw. "Yeah. That sound just about where I think it is. But ain't nobody been that deep in the woods in a long time. When we was kids, we used to go way back in there to hunt coons."

"Naw, there's a little road back off in there." Charlie closes his eyes and smiles, then opens his eyes and says, "You can't see it from the main road because ain't a lot of people going down that road. But it's there."

"A little ole dirt road?" Sho Boy asks.

"Yep," Charlie says.

Kenneth interrupts. "Y'all don't just wanna have Sol take us there through the woods?"

Charlie and Sho Boy shake their heads almost at the same time.

"If we get up there and it get hot. Ain't no way we gon' run through them woods and get away. They'a track us down and kill us right there in them woods," Sho Boy insists.

Charlie motions with his hands. "I can get us there. We'a cut through a short path and get in close enough. And we'a find it."

The men discuss guns and how they would approach the white men if they see them at the house. Charlie tells Kenneth several times that he should stay at home, but he refuses. Sho Boy suggests that they need one more person. Charlie tells him he'll see if Bo could come, because Willie's health isn't great. The men agree that Bo is just the right person because he is "slick with a gun," as Charlie says.

Sho Boy stares at Charlie. "Ain't no way you need to be out there in them woods. Hell, you can barely walk. They get out there on us, and we dead meat. Plus, we need Sol there to tell us where he came out them woods."

Charlie doesn't take this too kindly. "You think I'ma stay in the truck while y'all out there?"

"He's prolly right, Charlie," Kenneth says. "Won't you and Sol stay in the truck? We get out there, and if we ain't back by daybreak, then y'all drive on up that road to get us."

They plan to meet at Kenneth's house at ten o'clock, and they will all bring a gun with them. "All right Sol. Take care of ya self," the men say, before leaving.

I go into the barn and feed Simonton and Thunder. *This will be one night to remember. I hope nobody gets killed.*

CHAPTER TWENTY-FOUR

The sky is dark, and the wind comes with a piercing chill. Charlie's truck bounces from side to side over the rocky terrain, and the shocks squeak as the truck moves along the path leading to Movery's house. I'm squooshed between Charlie and Bo. Our torsos sway from side to side with the truck's bumpy movement. Just as the truck slows and comes to a stop, Kenneth and Sho Boy come out from the side of the house.

I hope I'm alive after tonight.

It took Charlie a long time to convince Mama to let me go, but she finally did after Charlie kept telling her, "Kat, we just gon' sit in the truck. We need him to tell us where the place is. He the only one that know how to get there."

My heart thumps when I see the men. Charlie turns the ignition switch, and the engine dies. Sho Boy walks to the passenger side window, and Bo turns the window crank and the window disappears into the door.

"Look what the wind den blowed in," Bo says, through his dark lips pressed tightly against his teeth.

Sho Boy drops his eyelids half-way and pushes his lips back. "Look atchu boy." Sho Boy throws two playful jabs at Bo, who swats them away.

"I ain't lost it, now," Bo grumbles.

They both grin. But those grins quickly subside and turn into blank faces on both men. "Good to see you Sho Boy." They bump fists.

Charlie opens his door. "Let's talk about what we gon' do."

The men gather next to a shed. There is a single light hanging from the roof, and I see three shotguns resting against the wall. Kenneth grabs one of the shotguns and tosses it to Charlie. "That's good enough for you?"

Charlie snatches the shotgun from mid-air and tilts his head, then allows his eyes to scan the barrel of the gun. "This here a thirty-one?"

Kenneth nods. "Yep. Remington. Got that side action." *Clack-clack.* Charlie pulls down on the action lever, then pushes it up. Kenneth tosses another shotgun to Bo. Bo catches the shotgun and holds it close by his side.

Kenneth then shoots a glance at Sho Boy. Sho Boy pulls his shirt up, and reveals a revolver pressed between his trousers and his waist. "I den already told you. I got my baby right here. She neva leave me."

Bo laughs. "Yeah, that bad boy got some mileage on it too."

Sho Boy bites down on the butt of a cigarette planted between his lips. "You ain't neva lied."

Sho Boy and Bo jump into the bed of the truck. Bo lays the shotgun on the bed, and Sho Boy sits with his back against the cabin and he pulls his hat down to cover his eyes. *We driving directly to hell.* Sweat forms on my back, and my shirt sticks to the leather seat. It takes a long time to get near the area. After making a few lefts, I guide Charlie to the location where I came out of the wood the day the white man shot at me.

"This it right here?" Charlie asks.

"Yeah. It's right there," I say, pointing at the exact spot. Charlie slows the truck.

"Damn, them woods is thick," Charlie says, hunching his shoulders forward. Charlie turns off the road into the shoulder and presses down on the gas to tread through the shrubbery, then pushes his head out of the window. "Is that good enough?"

"Go in a little mo'," Sho Boy says.

Charlie moves in closer to the woods.

"That's it. It's good right there," Bo yells.

Charlie and Kenneth exit the truck, while Sho Boy and Bo jump out of the bed. Charlie hands each man a helmet with a light attached at the front, and they form a small circle.

"Y'all gon' go about half a mile into there and then veer north when you get to the old cemetery, okay?" Charlie says. The men nod in agreement. "Me and Sol gon' be here waiting on y'all. If you ain't here by sunbreak, we hitting that road that lead to the house to come get y'all, hear me?"

"Yep. We gotchu," the men say at nearly the exact time and tone. The men start out and move into the woods. The three lights bounce on the greenish-brown vegetation, and I see them reach ahead and pull branches to the side, clearing the way to move through. Charlie and I sit quietly in the truck. I can't stop thinking about what's going on outside and what led us to this point.

"So, you wanna be a pilot, nephew?" Charlie says, breaking the silence.

"Yessir."

"What made you think about gettin' into something like that—somethin' that a man made and flying in the sky like a bird? Ain't you scared to be all the way up there and ain't nothing down here holdin' ya up?"

"Naw, no really."

"I ain't neva been in no plane and neva wanna be in one either. Hell, I get nervous even when I get on a John Brown train."

"You get scared on a train?"

Charlie chuckles. "Now, I ain't said nothin' about being scared. Scared and nervous are two different things. I ain't scared of nothin'."

I feel Charlie's spirit, and I believe every word he says. I've never seen him back down to nothing. Silence seeps into the truck again. Charlie lowers his chin. "If you see something wake me up. I'm just gon' close my eyes here fo' a minute."

"Uncle Charlie," I say, "have you ever seen my daddy before?" Charlie lifts his chin and stares through the windshield into darkness.

"Well, I heard about the situation, but I ain't really know much about it. You know, I know it must be hard not knowing yo' daddy. Yo' mama don't talk much about it. I figure she'a tell you mo' as you get older, but you...you a young man now. Don't make sense that you don't know nothin' about yo' daddy."

"You know anything about him?"

"Well, all I know is that Kat and some of her friends used to make trips out there to Mobile. They gotta lotta military men out there. Tell me, she fell head ova heels for one of 'em and she kept going back up there once or twice a month to see 'im. Now, we ain't neva seen him. He ain't neva came out or said nothin. Next thing you know, Kat pregnant and here comes my nephew."

I feel a rumbling in my chest, and I want to cry. "Has anybody seen him or know where he is?"

"Naw, not that I know of. I was up there in Mobile several years ago doing some work on the railroad, and I asked around. I heard through Kat's friends that his name was Simon. So, I went around to some of the bars there—but they said he had gone and nobody know where he went. So, I didn't pay it no mind after that. I just let it be."

My eyes fill with tears, but I press my face tight so that not one tear falls.

Charlie adjusts his shoulders back into the seat and pulls his hat down over his eyes. "I'ma shut my eyes for a minute, nephew."

"Okay, unc."

I wait for Charlie's snores to get louder and longer before I convince myself that he's in a dead sleep. I can't stand to sit in the truck and wait for the men to come back. *I want to help them, but I can't.* I pull on the door lever and it creaks, then I push the door out with my shoulder and it opens. Charlie moves slightly, but he's still asleep. Once outside, I reach behind the seat and pull out one of the shotguns, and gently push the door to close the opening without snapping it shut. The thick brush slows me down. I pull branches to the side and squeeze through the tight areas, making my way through the woods. When I reach the old cemetery, I move north and continue. When I realize I have traveled a few hundred yards past the cemetery, I spot smoke flowing into the air from a distance. *That's it.*

I creep slowly until I come within fifty yards of the house. Light from a vehicle's headlights flash clear across the yard and brighten the lower section of the woods. Two white men exit the truck and enter the house. From my far right, I see Kenneth and the men approach the porch with their guns drawn. When they get to the porch, Kenneth holds up one finger, signaling for the men to stay quiet. I feel adrenaline surge throughout my body. Kenneth stands in front of the door with Bo by his side. Sho Boy is several feet away near the trucks. Kenneth holds up three fingers this time and counts down ...*three, two, one.* He reaches, turns the doorknob, and pushes the door in. Bo and Kenneth move in with their rifles drawn. I move out of view and sprint to the back of the house. Light creeps through a seam in the wood planks. I sit the shotgun against the wall and look through to see what's going on inside. Kenneth and Bo have their guns pointed at three white men who are at a wooden table with large glass containers on top.

"You betta not move again, or I'll blow yo head off!" Bo yells.

The men raise their hands above their heads slowly. The husky built man says, "We ain't gon' move. Whatchall want?" he stutters. "Bo, why you gon' do this to us? We ain't did nothin' to y'all."

"Shut up!" Bo yells. By this time, Sho Boy makes his way into the house. The other two white men shift their heads to Sho Boy.

"Y'all can have whatever you want," the thin man says. "We'a let y'all just have it." He lowers one of his hands and points it at the wall full of bottles of moonshine.

"Didn't I tell you to shut up!" Bo yells again.

The thin man stands, and I get a side view of his face. He's Furly's brother, George. I've seen him at the store several times.

George gestures with his hands. "C'mon guys. We can think of another way to resolve this here." George insists, trying to persuade Bo. George places his palms on the table.

Sho Boy has his gun pointed directly at George. "He den already told ya now. You betta not move again."

George dismisses Sho Boy's advice and makes a quick move under the table.

Pow! A loud shot blares. The echo sends chills up my arms, and I turn my head from the wall and cover my ears with my hands. I hear George's body hit the floor. I look back through the seam and see George scrambling to the corner of the room. "Didn't I tell ya not to move," Sho Boy says, gritting his teeth, and standing near the doorway.

The other two men scamper to the back wall with their arms held high. George twists around on the floor. "I coulda killed ya. Next time, I ain't hitting ya shoulder, I'm going fo ya heart," Sho Boy says, with a deadly grin.

"Okay, okay..." George pleads, "whatchall want?"

Sho Boy nods to Kenneth. Kenneth lowers his gun, pulls out one of the chairs from the table, and sits. "Y'all had ma son in here. He say y'all was gon' hang 'im. And we ain't gon' let y'all do that."

Bo pans his gun from one man to another. "We ain't gon' hide the boy or nothin'. Somebody made a mistake, and he ended up in this here house. He ain't mean no harm, and we ain't gon' let y'all be killing us. So, y'all stay away from 'im, and you gon' promise that to us tonight."

Out of nowhere, *chak-chak*. The barrel of a shotgun appears behind Sho Boy's head. "Don't make a move," the deep voice utters from the porch. "I'll kill 'im right now. Y'all drop ya guns." Sho Boy's neck stiffens. He turns to the man, then takes side-steps into the house with his hands extended above his head. The man enters. He is tall and wearing dark clothing. "Y'all coming on our property and think you gon' threaten us?" he says, "that ain't happening. So, you gon' put ya guns down, or I'm gon' kill 'im right here on the spot."

My hands are sweaty and my legs tremble. Sho Boy lowers his gun, and Bo and Kenneth follow suit.

George stands. "That bastard shot me, and I'ma kill 'im." The other two men stand and pull guns from under the table. George rips his shirt and wraps his shoulder. The white men collect the rifles and Sho Boy's gun and put them into a large gunny sack. They command them to walk slowly out of the house. I sneak behind the truck with the shotgun cocked and ready to go.

The men force Bo, Kenneth, and Sho Boy to their knees and make them place their hands behind their heads. The other two white men stand on with their guns in hand.

The tall man takes charge. "Y'all had no bit'ness coming here and meddlin' with us. Who da hell ya think you are? Ain't no black man eva came 'round here demanding a damn thing from us. Tonight, y'all gon' learn ya selves a lesson," he says, standing near the front of the truck with his shotgun pointed downward.

As soon as the man raises the shotgun, I step from behind the truck and point the end of the barrel right to the side of his face. "Put the gun down," I bellow. "Don't think I won't shoot you dead right now." The tall man turns around. "Look..." I move the barrel to the sky swiftly and bang...I let off a shot, then yank on the action level quickly to reload. The man drops his gun. The other men on the porch stand. I keep my eyes on the tall man, but yell out, "Y'all better not take another step. The next one gon' be right in the side of his head. So, you betta drop your guns."

"Put ya guns down!" the tall man commands.

The men ease their guns onto the porch. Bo and Kenneth pick up the weapons and place them in the gunny sack with the other guns and carry them near the truck and drop the sack. "Go over there and sit on the porch wit' the other men," I tell the tall man.

The men sit on the porch, and Kenneth explains to them that they could've died. He has to convince Sho Boy to let the men live. *Bo don't want a race war on our hands.* Bo stands between Sho Boy and the men and whispers something in his ear.

"Y'all ain't gon' put ya hands on nobody, right?" Bo asks. "Nobody messin' withchall, so y'all don't mess with us. You understand?"

The men nod their heads.

Bo and Sho Boy tie the men up and take them back into the house. Kenneth slits the tires on the trucks before we leave so that the men can't catch us before we make it out of the woods.

Before leaving, Sho Boy grabs two glass jugs of moonshine. "I guess they won't be needing these no time soon," he says.

We walk through the woods and make it back to the truck before dawn. Charlie is leaning against the truck with his arms folded. *I have a lot to explain. But right now, all I can think about is getting some sleep.*

CHAPTER TWENTY-FIVE

Things are quiet around town. Mama keeps asking me to retell the story of what happened on that dreadful night, and each time I give her a few more details. I keep having nightmares of men coming on horses and taking me away. I've been able to make $23 dollars from catching coons and selling the fur to people around town. I gave Mama the money to put towards the $47 lien against the property, and we have less than thirty days to pay the balance in full. Willie tells me about a coon hunting contest that only takes one dollar to join and you can win up to fifty dollars. All I can think about is training Simonton for the contest.

We run Simonton in the woods with Redbone and and Bluetick a few times a week to get him ready. Willie is impressed with Simonton's speed and ability to pick up on scents, but he's worried that Simonton gets distracted easily. "If you don't fix that, he ain't gon' be no good coonhound. He'a be chasing foxes and rabbits and whatever else when he should be on that coon. You gotta break 'im of that," Willie says, with a hoarse sound and a nagging cough.

"How I do that?"

"Well, you gotta just keep him on it. Keep training him so he gets used to yo' voice more, and know if he don't do what you tell 'im, you gon' get 'im. That's the only way you can really train him." I listen attentively, nodding my head with every recommendation. Willie points at the dogs while they scramble around a tree. "Look like they picked up something. Look at 'em." Willie grins. The Redbone breaks away and trots farther into the woods. "Naw. I guess not. If ain't no coon there, she ain't wasting her time."

We follow the dogs at a slow pace. "You wanna talk about what happened in that place in the woods that night?"

I didn't realize I hadn't shared the story with Willie. "Well, it's a long story cut'n Willie."

Willie laughs. "Most good stories are," he says, "but I hear you saved ole Bo and your friend's daddy. I even heard ole Sho Boy was there."

"Yeah. It was a long night and a lot going on."

Willie stops and places his hand on my shoulder. "Look. You'a good kid. I ain't neva had no kids—let alone a son. So, alls I can tell you is...you gotta know that life ain't nothin' but a chess game, son. You eva played chess?"

"Nosir," I reply, feeling some intrigue about knowing more.

"Okay. You got this king, right? And the whole goal is for all the pieces on the board to protect the king—now, that's not saying the other pieces cain't move on the board and be a part of the game, but they just ain't the king. You wit' me?"

"Yessir."

"In this here," Willie extends his arm to his side and twists his torso, "I'm a king. Them two hounds there will fight to they death to protect me. But when I leave these here woods, I ain't no king. I'm on somebody else's board. "That make sense?"

"Yessir," I say, with little apprehension.

Willie's grin widens. "It'll start making sense to you one day, son."

***

On a cool and crisp morning, I wake up at dawn to feed Thunder and Simonton. I unlatch the door on the barn door and enter. Simonton howls and is antsy.

"Mo'nin, Mister Thunder. Time to eat." There is silence in the stall. I pick up some fodder and continue. "Oh. You gon' be quiet today, huh?" I don't hear a sound from the stall. I climb on the gate, peer over, and see my horse lying flat on the ground. "Thunder!" I yell. Tears stream down my face. I run to the house to tell Mama.

"Thunder is dead," I yell. Mama is standing in the kitchen stirring contents in a pot.

"No!" she screams, frowning and uttering the single word laced with pain. The spoon drops from her hand to the floor. She darts by me and through the door.

"I'ma go get Uncle Charlie," I yell in her direction. I turn back and see Mama running to the barn as I head to the main road. I swing my arms and move my feet fast without breaking stride. When I finally get to Charlie's house, he's on the front porch slipping on his boots. He must sense that I'm in distress.

"What's the matter?"

"Thunder dead."

Charlie sits up from the chair. He glances at me. "You okay, nephew?" I feel a tingling in my fingers, and I can't say a word. "Stay right there. I'a be right back." Charlie goes into the house and comes back out with a heavy coat. "Let's go." We get into the truck and leave.

When we get to the house, Mama is sitting on the porch and knitting.

"Hey, sis," Charlie says.

Mama's head doesn't move. "Hey, Charlie."

Charlie and I make it to the barn. He stands on the lowest board on the gate and looks into the stall. "Yeah. He definitely gone." Charlie steps down from the gate. "So, I reckon y'all wanna bury him around here somewhere?"

I nod.

"Won't you gon' in there witcho mama, and I'll take care of it."

"No, unc. I'ma help you."

"Okay. Where you wanna bury 'im?"

"Right on the other side of the garden. Right over there where he used to plow. That's the best place."

Charlie and I dig a big hole and bury Thunder later that afternoon. *I'ma miss my horse.*

CHAPTER TWENTY-SIX

The pain of losing an animal hurts me at the core, and whenever I think about Thunder, I feel a swelling in my throat. The excitement of running coons or going fishing has escaped me. My sheer desire is to sit around the farm and fling rocks into the pasture and watch them whizz through the air. I dream of one day leaving here, gone, and never blinking an eye when someone asks if I want to go back. I want to get as far away as I can from this dreadful place. One day, I'll be able to fly in the skies and go wherever I want. *I don't even know who my daddy is.*

While these deep thoughts run through my head, I see Willie's truck pull off the road and head toward the house. I get up from my somber mood and take exhausting steps in the direction of the truck. Willie sits behind the wheel with a broad grin, looking at me through the window.

"Where Simonton at?"

"In the barn," I say, as dry as I can.

"What's gotten into you?"

"Nothin."

"Naw. Something must've gotten into you. You know...I heard ya horse died, and I wanna let you know I'm sorry to hear that."

"Yeah. He was old. I guess that's what happens when you get old."

Willie chuckles. "Well, getting old ain't so bad. If you get to be old, then that's a blessing, right?"

"I guess."

"Hey. Did y'all ever sign Simonton up for that contest?"

"Not yet. I don't have no money. Last bit of money I had we had to pay them people 'cause they tryna take our property."

"Let's go get ole Simonton signed up for that contest."

"For real?"

"Yes. For real. Get on in here. Let's go get 'im in this contest."

I hop into the passenger seat of the truck, and we pull off. Willie drives with one hand at the very top of the steering wheel and the other one relaxed with his elbow on top of the interior of the window. "How far is Mobile from here?" I ask.

"It's a coupla hours—ain't too far, why?"

"I don't know." I wipe the sweat from my forehead with my hand.

"Well, seem like you either ain't knowing much today or you ain't tryna say nothin. No matter which one it is, you gon' have to talk about it. If not, it's gon' stay on yo' chest. Now, that's one thing old people know about."

I giggle. "All right, all right. So, Uncle Charlie tell me my daddy was in the Navy and met my mama in Mobile, and I guess that's…"

"Um-hmm," Willie responds.

"And that's how I got here, I guess."

Willie tilts his head to the side and looks out into the sky. "Okay. I see how that can eat chu up from the inside. 'Cause you don't even know who he is, huh?"

"Nope. And I ain't neva seen him or nothin'. All I seen is pictures of 'im—that's it, just pictures."

"That's okay."

"What do you mean *that's okay*?"

"The Lord gon' take care of that too, just like he do everything else. You just gotta wait on him, young man."

I shake my head, trying to wrap my brain around things that have never quite made sense to me. "So, how the Lord gon' take care of that?"

"Well, that's what we gotta believe, no matter how tough things get."

My mind is flustered, running like a roaring riptide, but when Willie talks, I feel a calmness creep into my mind like a switch that controls my flow of thoughts.

We get to Furly's and there's another man at the counter.

"Can we talk to Furly?" Willie asks the man.

"Well, how can I help you?" the man says.

"I wanna talk to Furly."

The man's eyes tighten, and his face turns pinkish like a dried strawberry. "Wait right here." He turns and moves through the door behind the counter. A few seconds later, Furly appears from the room.

"Hey, Sol. And Willie, how y'all doing?" Furly's eyes stay on me longer than normal. I turn my head, wondering is he's trying to make me out as the person he shot at.

"Just fine there, Mister Furly. We just come down here to register Sol's hound in that coon contest that's coming up soon," Willie says, "you know, the one that costs a dollar to join."

Furly shifts his eyes to me. "The contest?"

"Yessir," I say.

Furly takes a long sigh, and I feel the air from his nose. "What?" Furly says to Willie, "you gon' have one of yo' coonhounds in the contest? 'Cause you know they gotta be full-blooded or else they cain't be the contest."

I nudge Willie. "See, that's what I'm talking about. Let's go."

Willie looks down at me. "Naw cut'n, we all right. I'm just gon' talk to Mister Furly a little mo'." Willie raises his chin and plants his eyes back on Furly. "So, we feel like his dog Simonton need to be in this contest, and that's what we want."

Furly stares Willie down and fidgets with a coin in his hand. "Well, that ain't happening," Furly says, "don't matter what you want. He ain't getting in that contest."

"Let's go cut'n Willie," I interject.

Willie turns to me and spreads a comforting smile across his face. "We ain't going nowhere," he says, then reaches deep into his pant pocket, "now, you go on over there and getchu some of that candy while I talk to Mister Furly here."

"But..."

"Naw, you gon' getchu a few pieces, and we'a be done inna few minutes."

I move along the aisles of the store, trying to eavesdrop on what Willie and Furly are talking about, but I'm too far away. I see Willie gesturing with his hands and Furly standing in the same position, just staring at Willie.

After a while, Willie turns to me. "C'mon here, Sol. Let's get this thing taken care of." Furly steps into the back room, and when he returns, he's carrying a manila envelope.

"Just fill out the paperwork," Furly says, then pushes the documents across the counter at Willie.

"Why, thank you, sir," Willie says.

I turn to Willie and give him one of the biggest smiles ever. Willie winks back.

***

Willie and I train Simonton over the next two weeks. We make sure he doesn't veer from coon trails. It's hard for me to whack him across the head at first, but it becomes easier because I know how important it is for him to stay locked on coon trails.

The night before the contest, I ask Mama to join me for prayer. I kneel on the floor in my room with Mama right next to me. We read Psalms 91, and when we end, Mama hugs me and thanks God for such a wonderful son.

"Now, I don't want you worrying about that twenty-five dollars, son. That's not for you to worry about. We gon' make it," she says, "okay?"

"Yes, ma'am."

"Now, you listen to Charlie when you down there. Them people might be looking all atchu on the cause of me pulling that gun on that man, but you just pray, okay?"

"Yes." I nod my head, but deep down inside I can't think about nothing else other than walking into that office and paying off the bill. *I want to see Mama happy. Me and Simonton gon' win this contest.*

CHAPTER TWENTY-SEVEN

I can't wait.

I've never seen this many boys and dogs together at the same time. "Wow Charlie. You see all these dogs?" I pull my back away from the seat of the truck to get a closer view of the dogs through the smeared windshield. Simonton dances around in the bed of the truck, antsy and ready for the challenge. The wooden sign posted at the entrance reads: 1944 Sumerville Coonhunting Challenge. Everyone is gathering near a table at the edge of the woods.

Charlie parks the truck. I hop out, then whip around to the bed of the truck. "Comere boy." Simonton springs off the tailgate and I kneel next to him. He's breathing heavy and his chest moves in and out fast with his tongue dangling from his mouth. "This what we been waitin' for boy. I need you to go out there and do your best.

185

You hear me?" Simonton yelps for me as if he understands every word I'm saying. "There you go. You know what I'm talkin' about."

Charlie watches on. "Man, it's a lot of people here today."

"You think Willie coming?" I ask.

"I'm not sure. We neva know. Ole Willie will prolly be here."

"Okay," I say, "y'all gotta see Simonton at work."

Charlie laughs. "Yeah. We gon' see him at work."

I wrap the leash around Simonton's neck and walk him to the path leading to the table. Almost all of the boys are white, though I do see a couple of black boys walking around with their parents, but they don't have dogs. The howling of the dogs gets me excited. I see a brown Plott Hound strut by with his master. His nose is on the ground, and he's sniffing like he picked up a scent already. Simonton tugs on the leash like he wants to get after the dog, but I pull back on the leash. "Hold boy." Simonton lets up. The curious stares from the people add to my anxiety as I get in line for the check-in.

Furly stands behind the table with his arms folded and he keeps checking his wristwatch. The man from Furly's store sits at the table and he's wearing a brown cap that matches his khaki trousers, and a short sleeve vest that hugs his body tightly. Another younger man stands beside him with a tag around his neck and a white sheet of paper on his chest that has the word "Judge" scribbled in pencil across it. He smiles nervously as he looks from dog to dog.

I twist my body a full 360 degrees and see the dogs that have already checked, and they are eager to get into the woods. Any one of them can be one of the dogs that I've seen in the magazines. Their coats are shiny and each one meticulously groomed.

I begin to lean from one foot to another, feeling the excitement swell in me just like the first day I got Simonton. I look to my side and Simonton is hale and hearty, wagging his tail in the air and eyeing the pack of dogs standing on a stretch of grass whose names had been called and they had been verified. The sun is out but there are clouds blocking it from blaring down hard on the woods. A gentle breeze makes the tree leaves sway in the air and carries along with it the pleasant smell of the forest.

"Next," the man says.

Simonton and I move to the table. The judge reviews the papers and squints his eyes as he inspects Simonton closely.

"This here is a English Coonhound?" he asks.

"Yessir," I respond quickly.

"I never seen one like this. Wait here a minute." The judge stands and heads in Furly's direction, holding the papers away from his body. Charlie and I watch on.

"Don't worry nephew. Why you panicking? I told you it's gon' be okay."

Furly converses with the judge, looks in our direction, and nods. The judge walks back to the table.

"Okay, you're fine."

I smile and hurry to the area where the other dogs are anxiously awaiting to get started. I wrap Simonton's decal around his torso. He's number 37. Amidst the raucous yelps and howls, Simonton is quiet. He looks up at me, and for the first time, I see fear in his eyes.

"What's wrong boy?" I kneel next to him again. Simonton scratches at my chest with his paws, wanting me to pick him up just like I did when he was a puppy. "Naw, boy. It's gon' be okay. You can do it." I push him away and he moans.

Furly walks into the grassy area. "Okay. I want to thank

everybody for coming out here today. Thank you for your patience in checking in and everythang. We wanted to make sure all your dogs have been properly registered, verified, and ready to go. Now, I been telling y'all for a while that this is a single shot contest. We got scorers all out there in them woods waiting to tally things up when your dogs tree a coon. Now, we don't have no idea how many coons out there, but your dog got his number around his body and when he tree a coon, he gotta have his legs on the trunk, if not, he won't get no points. You can try your best to follow your dog through the woods but know that there's a lot of you and it might get crazy out there. The competition will last three hours. After the run, we will come back here and tally things up and see who the winner is. Last thing, if your dog is not the one that tree the coon first, but he there, he will get a half point as long as he on that trunk. And when they hit a tree and ain't no coon up there, he won't get no deduction. He just wasting his own time."

There is a chorus of laughs in the crowd.

Furly continues. "So, you better get 'im off that tree and on to a real trail." Furly pulls a whistle to his mouth. "If there ain't no questions, all I'ma do is blow this whistle here, and at that time you gon' let yo' dog off his leash. But don't let him off 'til you hear this whistle, 'cause if you let 'im off early, he gon' be disqualified," he says. "Nah, y'all understand me?"

"Yes," we all say at once.

Furly blows the whistle, and the dogs all start out, scrambling into the woods and howling like a wild bunch of wolves while Furly and the nervous judge follow behind the owners.

"Go get 'im boy," I yell out to Simonton. He's out in front of the other hounds, and I smile broadly when I hear Simonton's howl amidst the chaos. Simonton catches a trail and moves on it quickly. His nose moves along the ground, his tail wags in the air, and he darts through the thickets and disappears. I follow Simonton's deep howl and yell, "Get on 'im boy. There you go."

I watch in delight as Simonton follows hard on a coon trail until he comes to a shallow stream that runs along a steep hill. Simonton hits the tree first, with a Bluetick close on his back legs. Simonton raises his front legs on the trunk of the hickory and howls his treeing bark. There is a scorer nearby who hears Simonton's howl and moves to his bark. I see Simonton through the brush and pull the shrubs to the side to move through. "Good boy. Talk to me. Talk to me." Simonton howls loudly. "You got 'im?" Simonton howls again.

The scorer looks high into the tree and spots the coon.

"That's a hit. Great job, number thirty-seven." The scorer scribbles on the paper and marks the tree. The owners of the two other dogs stand beside Simonton, watching on.

"Comere boy." Simonton stops barking and sprints to me. I give him a piece of bacon, then pull him away from the tree. I point in the opposite direction. "Scat now!" Simonton turns and runs in the direction of where I point, and gets on another trail.

"He's quick," the scorer says.

Simonton runs through the brush and leaps over a small creek. I'm several yards behind Simonton when he picks up on another trail. He howls again. I throw my arms in the air. "Yes!" Simonton gets to a short elevation and stops, looks around, and picks up the scent again. He howls louder. *He ain't getting away from Simonton. He must be hiding.* Simonton moves around a small rock and growls. I hear a high-pitch snarl that sounds like a coon. Simonton howls again. I finally catch up with my dog. "Get 'im boy. Talk to me." Simonton stands near the rock and howls again.

Another scorer hears the howls and comes within a short distance from the rocks. "Is this your dog?"

"Yessir."

"Look like he got one. All's I'ma do is see if the coon is between them rocks. If I see 'im, your dog get a point."

"Get 'im boy," I yell out again, and Simonton moves in closer to the rock. Simonton growls, shows his teeth, and inches closer to the rocks. The coon snarls loudly.

The scorer makes a note on the clipboard. "You got it."

I give Simonton another treat and send him on to the next trail. He's doing well. Within only an hour, we have already scored four clear points. I grin from ear to ear. On his fifth trail, Simonton picks up on a scent and it takes us far away from the other dogs. I hear him from a distance, but his bark is losing its strength. I swing my arms and legs as quickly as I can to make up ground, but Simonton is moving farther and farther away. *I'm exhausted.*

I sit for a moment to catch my breath then call out to Simonton, "Aha-Aha-Aha." Moments later, Simonton's bark becomes stronger and stronger, which is a sign that he is running in my direction.

Another scorer hears the barks and moves near me. "Is that your dog?"

"Yes. Seems like he's on another one."

Simonton howls loudly. "Get 'im boy," I yell out to Simonton. Simonton howls again. The scorer moves with me through the thick brush. When we get to an open space, we see Simonton with his legs planted on a tree trunk and he howls louder when he sees me. Simonton scores again.

After I give him a treat, I send him away to get on another

trail. This time, Simonton follows two other hounds and all three are in hot pursuit. Just as they get to a shallow stream of water, Simonton stops abruptly and veers off. He takes a few quick sniffs on the ground and looks in the opposite direction. I see him from a distance and bend over to take a breath. "Whatchu see boy?" I say, while catching my breath. I had seen Simonton do this several times. "Come here!" I yell. Simonton's tail wags and he jets in the opposite direction. "Simonton!" I scream. Simonton leaps through the branches and doesn't respond to my commands. I trail him as close as I can, but Simonton sprints at nearly full speed.

When Simonton gets to the edge of the woods, he shoots across a huge pasture and howls. I hear the howls and keep running in the direction of his bark. I cross a corn field and at the end there is an opening. I see Old Man Micah and Sara, and they standing at the edge of the last line of corn. Sara is shaking, and Micah stands in front of the her, shielding her from a wild boar who is foaming at his mouth and chomping his jaws. Simonton creeps slowly into the opening and growls at the boar. Micah raises a stick and tries to shoo the boar away, but it only agitates him more. The boar sees Simonton and switches his attention to him. Simonton growls more intensely and shows his teeth. "Simonton," I yell again. The boar turns, faces Simonton, and groans. Simonton stands his ground. The couple watches on in fear.

Simonton attacks the boar and sinks his teeth into the back of his neck. The boar squeals and yanks his body, throwing Simonton off him. He then attacks Simonton and catches him between his shoulders and neck and swings Simonton around. Simonton yelps, falls to the ground, and lies on his back. The boar charges him again and just as he's about to rip at Simonton's back, Simonton lunges up and clamps on to his neck. The boar tussles with Simonton and finds a way to claw at his torso and sink his teeth into the back of Simonton's neck. Blood rushes through my body, and I'm feeling faint.

The couple screams, "Get off of him!" The boar's strength is too much for Simonton, and he yanks him around so aggressively that Simonton's body is going limp, he's not fighting back. My breaths are heavy, and the images flood my mind. I see my dog's blood smeared on the green grass, and I hear a loud yelp from Simonton, then it fades quickly. "No!" I scream. I reach into my pocket, pull out my knife, and charge the boar. When I get closer, I reach back and swing my arm sharply at the boar's chest. I feel the knife drive into his flesh. He squeals loudly. Blood squirts out and splatters on my arm. I pull the knife out and strike again with successive stabs until the boar's chest no longer moves. I push the heavy boar to the side. Blood drips from my shirt.

Simonton lay on his side and pants. "You okay, boy?" I cry. The couple stands by, and they are speechless. "No, you not gon' die on me, boy. You gotta get up," I yell. "Somebody help me!"

One of the scorers enters the area. "My God. What happened?" He kneels next to Simonton. "Let's sew him up. This is pretty bad." Simonton lies helpless. His breathing slows, and he blinks his eyes. The scorer pulls out a small first aid kit from his jacket and threads a needle.

"You know how to do this?" he asks.

"Yeah," I nod. I start on the deep cut under Simonton's neck. I push the needle into Simonton's flesh, and he jerks away. "It's okay boy. Hold on, let me take care of this." Simonton's blood runs down my arm every time I raise my hand to make another loop. I'm so focused on stopping the bleeding that I don't even think about wiping his blood away. Simonton ain't moving, and my heart drops.

CHAPTER TWENTY-EIGHT

Furly arrives at the scene with two other men, and one of them leads the couple away as he and I stand over Simonton and watch his eyes blinking weakly. Furly places his finger on the side of Simonton's neck. "He's alive," he says, "but we gotta get him to a doctor fast."

I gather Simonton into my arms carefully and lift him up. He's heavy, so Furly helps me by grabbing his lower body. We walk briskly through the woods for several minutes, angling my dog's body through stringy tree branches and balancing, so that we don't fall and make things worse. When we get to a clear opening, Furly stops.

"Let's just lay him down right here," Furly says. He then reaches into his pocket and tosses keys to the scorer. "Take these and run back to the starting area and get my truck." Furly then points. "Bring it right around the edge of that thick brush near that long curve and cut across and you'll end up right there near the main road, and we'a be there. You know what I'm talkin' 'bout?"

The scorer bobbles his head and says, "Yessir." He then sprints away.

"C'mon. Let's take him this way," Furly says. Furly and I pick him up to carry him to the main road. When we get near the road, we see the truck and it's moving fast. It pulls off the road and slows when it gets close to me and Furly. The scorer jumps out of the truck. I pull the tailgate down and we all grab a part of Simonton and lift him into the back of the truck. Furly moves to the driver's seat, and I jump on the back of the truck.

"I'ma stay back here," I yell.

"Okay," Furly replies.

I hold on to Simonton and whisper into his ears, making new promises and reaffirming old ones as the truck speeds along the road. The truck pulls into a large farm wrapped in a white picket fence, and I see a man pushing a shovel into the ground. The man adjusts to an upright position and places a hand over his eyes, shielding them from the blaze of the sunlight as the truck pulls over. Furly pushes the door open and steps out. "Stay right there," Furly says, while turning from me and approaching the man.

"You gon' be all right, boy. You gon' be all right," I say into Simonton's ear. The blood on his face has dried with the wind of the ride, but the gash in his neck still bleeds through the stitches. I listen on to what Furly is saying to the man.

"We've got a situation here, doc. The dog was attacked by a wild boar, and he lost a lot of blood."

"When did this happen?" the man asks, and pulls a handkerchief from his trousers' pocket.

"Just a couple of minutes ago," Furly answers, "in the woods."

The man wipes his face with the handkerchief and stares at me with a piercing frown. "Now, whose dog is it?"

"It's the boy's dog," Furly answers, pointedly. "Like I said, doc, the dog is bleeding, and would probably need some stitches. And I think one of the bones in his right leg is broken."

The man slowly folds the handkerchief back while fixing his eyes on me. "I'm sorry." He picks his words carefully as he returns the handkerchief into his pocket. "But I won't be rendering my services to that boy there. Maybe you can find someone else in town who would agree to treat 'im," he states firmly.

"You will work on the dog!" Furly snaps back. "It's just a dog for goodness sake!"

"No, I ain't. And you should think about where you stand too, John."

"Look, doc, I know where I stand. This dog saved old man Micah and Sara from a wild boar, and I am telling you right now that I am not leaving these premises until you treat the dog!"

The man turns and starts to walk away and Furly follows him.

"He is a registered dog," Furly says, as if this is a threat. "You gon' turn your back on a registered dog?" Furly laughs. "Go on, then, doc. Walk away from a registered dog and let's see if anyone will be standing with you after the entire state of Alabama hears about it." His voice drips with sarcasm. The man stops walking, turns, and faces Furly. "You know what will happen, don't you? You'll lose every bit of business in town, that's what. And you won't find another client nowhere in these parts."

SOL & SIMONTON

The man raises his hand. "Enough!" he says. He looks at me with Simonton clutched in my arms. "Bring him to the side house."

"Thank you very much, sir," I say. Furly and I pick up Simonton and follow the man into the building next to the house. As we arrive at the front steps, the man turns to me and frowns. "Ain't no colored folk entering my house." He stands and blocks the doorway.

Furly turns to me and collects Simonton into his arms. "It's all right, Sol. I will take him in," he says, and smiles. "You can wait in the truck, and I'll take you home. It may take a while before it's all done."

"Can I sleep in the barn and wait?" I ask and turn to the man with imploring eyes. "Please, sir."

Mr. Furly turns to the man and waits for his response.

He looks exasperated, and after a long pause, he nods. "You can stay in the barn, but don't disturb those animals."

Furly reassures me. "You just stay put," he says, "your dog will be all right."

"Thank you, Furly."

Furly carries Simonton into the side house. I drop my head and take a slow pace to the barn. I see a truck exit the road and pull into the long driveway. It's Charlie and Mama. Mama's door swings open before the truck comes to a stop. Her feet drop to the ground, and she runs directly to me.

"You okay?"

I shake my head, but I feel tears filling my eyes. "I'm okay."

"Where's Simonton?"

"The doctor took him in that building and he working on 'im."

"What doctor?" Charlie asks.

"I dunno. Furly just brought me here. I don't even know 'im."

Mama's eyes are tight. "Where Furly at?"

"He back there with 'im."

She points. "In that building ova there?"

"Yeah. That's it." I get scared whenever Mama fire off questions like this.

"C'mon, Charlie," she says, "let's go get the dog."

"Wait Mama. We can't go get 'im now. He in bad shape."

She turns to me and allows her eyes to pinch me with a bitter stare, and she shakes her head to add to her agitation. "C'mon here, Charlie. Sol, you stay right here and we'a be back."

"No. I'm goin'," I say matter-of-factly, staring right back at her.

Mama's face loosens. "Okay. Let's go."

Charlie knocks on the door. It opens and the doctor stands in the doorway.

"Can I help you?" he muffles through the mask.

"We're here to pick up the dog," Mama says.

"Pick the dog up?" he asks.

By this time, Furly moves into the doorway. "Eve-ning, Kat," Furly says. "You say you comin' to pick up the dog?"

"Yeah. We here to pick 'im up."

"He ain't in no kinda shape to be moved, Kat. He in bad shape. 'Bout time you get 'im in that truck and move 'im, he'a probably die."

"Well, that's just a chance we gotta take," Mama says.

Simonton is heavily bandaged, and he's not moving. Charlie pulls the truck as close as he can to the building, and we load Simonton onto the back of the truck. My hands shake, and I hope the ride won't be too much for him to bear.

"Where we takin' 'im?" I ask Charlie right before he slams the tailgate closed.

"We gon' take 'im to Willie's. He'a know what to do."

SOL & SIMONTON

When we get to Willie's, he's standing near his barn, and there is light glowing from the inside. *I bet Mama and Charlie had already planned this with Willie.* Charlie swings the truck around and backs the end into the entrance of the barn. Redbone and Bluetick come howling at us. "Get back," Willie yells. The dogs retreat.

Willie guides Charlie with his hands. "'Lil mo', 'lil mo...okay, right there." Charlie stops just short of the truck bed entering through the wide door. Charlie turns off the engine and gets out. Mama is wide-eyed and pacing near the back of the truck. Willie slowly approaches and lets off a hacking cough. "Looks like ole Simonton den been inna war," he says.

I feel a lump rising in my chest, and my eyes water again. "Can you help him cut'n Willie?" Willie smiles, but it is interrupted by another series of coughing.

"You okay?" Mama asks.

"Yeah. I'm okay. It just gotta run through me. I'a be okay," Willie says. "Look like Simonton ain't doing okay, though. We'a get 'im right. I'ma need Charlie and Sol to ease 'im off that truck. Don't be tryna move fast either. Get 'im over there on that bed, and I can start working on 'im."

We get Simonton and gently place him on the bed that Charlie made for him in the barn. Willie checks his temperature and moves his hand along different areas of his body. He lowers his ear and listens, while tapping along his legs and his chest while we all look on.

"Sol, you gon' stay here?" Mama asks.

Willie raises his chin. "Y'all can all go into the house and stay if you want. I got plenty of peas in there I made and some chicken... cornbread—y'all help ya'selves."

"I wanna stay out here with Simonton and Willie," I say.

Mama nods in agreement. "What about you Charlie?"

"Them peas and chicken sound good right about now."

Mama's exhaustion only allows one side of her lip to form a smile and a slight chuckle. "Okay. I'ma go on in the house." Mama steps away and moves through the door.

Willie is still poking and prodding on Simonton's body while I look on at his every move. I lay on top of a haystack and let my head relax on its side. The next morning, I'm awakened by the opening of the barn door and light splashes directly onto my face. I'm balled up with my head resting on a batch of hay. My face is covered in morning sweat, and as soon as my eyes adjust to the bright light, I see Willie standing with Mama and Charlie.

"Wake up, son!" Mama says. Charlie claps his hands. "We gotta take Simonton home."

I turn my head slowly and dust off my shirt. "Where Simonton?" I ask quickly, and look beyond the three of them, searching for my dog.

Charlie smiles. "Relax. He still ova there in that bed."

Simonton is lying flat on the bed, but his eyes are open. Tears settle in my eyes. "Simonton," I yell.

"Hold...hold," Willie says, "ole Simonton gon' hear yo' voice and try to get up."

"Oh, I'm sorry."

Willie walks to the bed and rubs Simonton's neck. "He lost a lotta blood. Look like that boar caught him across the chest and just ripped out the muscle across his breastplate. That's my biggest worry. Once we get this temperature down, he'a be okay. But he ain't gon' be chasing no coons no time soon."

"So, you think he gon' live?" I ask.

"Uh. I think he'a be okay, but that fever is what I'm worried about. Let him stay here a few days, and I'a watch him to make sure it go down. But I stitched 'im up real good, and it don't look like there's no infection or nothin'."

I exhale. "Thank you, cut'n Willie."

"Awe, no need to mention it. I hear Simonton went out there and got on them coons real good, huh?"

"Yeah. He treed like five, and no other dog was close to 'im." Willie giggles. "Then he saw the boar and ole man Micah…"

"Yeah. Cain't question his bravery at all," Willie says, "and I hear you took care of that boar to end it all," Willie adds, with a proud grin.

"Yessir."

Mama and Charlie leave and go home. There's no way I'm leaving my dog by himself. I sit around the barn all day, just reading the magazines and newspapers that Willie gives me.

When the sun falls, I get on my knees and pray. I ask God to give him more time to live.

CHAPTER TWENTY-NINE

It takes Simonton a whole week before he even tries to stand on his own. He moans and yelps throughout the day and night, and it pains me to see him suffer like this. So many people from town stop by just to see him. They are calling me and Simonton heroes after saving Old Man Micah and Sara from the boar, but a part of me is empty because he was on his way to win the contest, and now he's suffering.

Mama got a letter in the mail for us to go to a special meeting at Sumerville Town Hall. Sumerville always has town meetings, but me and Mama have never attended any of them, and she never felt the need; not that the colored folks are given much attention anyway. Most of the decisions concerning the town are made in the meetings, and some of the government officials are always present.

Charlie picks us up and we head to the meeting. When we enter the hall, the crowd starts whispering behind us. There are seats reserved for us. Mama glances at me, and it feels good to sit amongst important people and wear my crisp, blue shirt and my new, black trousers.

My eyes follow Mama's gaze to the front of the hall, and behind the two tables placed before the crowd sits George Furly beside a fat man who wears a suit and tie with a grim look and demeanor that suggests he is a government official. Five other members of the town council sit behind the tables. George cuts his eyes at me but I know he'll never want the world to know why his shoulder is really bandaged up.

The fat man stands and calls for some decorum, and the hall falls silent.

"That's the mayor," Charlie whispers to me and I nod slowly. "You ain't seen him before, have ya?"

I shake my head slowly and keep my gaze straight ahead.

"We are here gathered today, in this here meeting, to discuss the affairs of Sumerville and choose people who are gonna be members of the wildlife and forest watch committee," the mayor states, and the crowd murmurs. "But before we go into all that, we will celebrate one of Sumerville's finest young people."

I adjust myself in my seat and glance nervously at Mama sitting beside me. Mama smiles at me and nods.

"We'd like to call on Mister Perkins and Sara Johnson to come forward," the mayor says. "Now, for folks who don't know already, Micah Perkins and Sara were attacked by a wild boar in the woods. We know we've had our share of attacks lately and folks kinda been on edge. It ain't a good thing to come home and see that them wild boar den ate up all your chickens or killed some of your pigs—now I'm being a little facetious here, but y'all know what I'm talking about, don't you?"

The crowd murmurs loudly, and I hear some gasps.

"But they were saved by a dog, which couldn't be here today, because he suffered some damage to his body while defending Micah and Sara," the mayor continues as Sara escorts Micah to the front of the hall.

Old Man Micah turns to me as they pass beside my row of chairs, and he gives me a smile. I smile back and nod quickly. The mayor smiles at the couple as they walk to the front of the hall and stand beside him.

"Micah has been in this town longer than anybody, and we are happy to have him and Sara here safe and sound today. All thanks to that dog and Simon Canning," he says. "Now, as one of the first colored men to get employed here in this town a long time ago, we are proud of that. And we want people to know that our town ain't just about seeing people just because of their skin color." The mayor turns to the crowd. "In what way are we gonna reward this act of bravery and sense of duty?"

The crowd whispers their suggestions amidst themselves, and one man shouts aloud, "Get him a good fat bone." Just about everyone in the hall laughs, and I even smile despite my nervousness.

"That's right, Mister Emerson," the mayor says, "we are definitely going to have to give the dog a good fat reward." The crowd laughs again. The mayor looks serious again, and he takes a step forward. "What this dog has done to save the lives of Micah and Sara is what the founding fathers of this country fought for, and it is what our national anthem says, 'the home of the brave' and

I'd like to commend this dog and his master for being strong and fighting off a wild boar that was twice his size and certainly more powerful. And today, we want to celebrate them both." He takes a pause, then continues. "They killed a vicious enemy," he adds, then glances around the crowd as if he's looking for something until a round of applause goes round the hall.

The mayor then steps back and picks up a paper from the table. "I will now call up the owner of the dog, a true hero of Sumerville, Mr. Simon Solomon Canning."

The crowd claps, and I stand and walk to the mayor. I take a brief glance at George, and he starts a slow clap that eventually gets in rhythm with the crowd. *That was awkward.*

"This young man was there when the dog attacked the boar. When the boar kinda got the best of the dog, this young man jumped in and finished him off," the mayor says, as he shakes my hand. "Thank you very much, son," he says, then points, "look at the camera." Old Man Micah and Sara stand beside me, and we pose for the camera. The flash flares bright and I squint my eyes.

"As a show of gratitude for his service to this town, Micah and Sara, and the town council will like to reward you with this," the mayor announces, and hands me a large parcel.

I take it and smile quickly as the light of the camera flashes again. The crowd claps, and some men stand and walk me back to my seat with the prize in my hands. Mama grips my hand and we smile at each other. Charlie gives me a tight fist and a wink. "Top man!" he says.

On the way home, Mama can't stop smiling. She keeps saying, "My son a hero." Every time she says it, I feel butterflies dance in my stomach.

"Thanks for everything, uncle." I say, while exiting the truck.

"See you later, Chuck," Mama says.

"All right, sis." Charlie leans out of the driver's side window as he pulls off. "My nephew a hero. Good God, a real life hero." The truck turns and disappears into the night.

"Can I open it?" I ask Mama as soon as we enter the house. She lights two candles.

"Yeah. Let's see what's in there."

I smile and look up at Mama with beseeching eyes as I hold the parcel.

Mama pulls off one of her shoes. "Come on boy, hurry up."

I peel off the parcel string until it reveals a large, untitled black book, and resting in the center of the book, is the edge of a one-hundred-dollar bill. Excitement rushes through my body. "Mama. It's a one-hundred-dollar bill." Mama rushes to my side and her eyes grow wide. "I have never seen one of those before," she says, "what a blessing."

"We have a hundred dollars, mama."

"I told you God will reward good people." Mama smiles at me and sinks into her chair in high spirits.

I kneel beside Mama. "This is for you, mama." I press the bill into her hand. "Thank you for everything, mama." Mama looks back at me with an empty stare with her mouth gaped open. She doesn't know what to say.

"It's yours, son. You should keep it," she finally mumbles through the lump of emotion in her throat.

"No, mama, this is yours," I say and stand, "thank you for taking care of me, and Simonton too. You always do your best to provide for us. And I wanna give Willie some of it too. I'ma ask Charlie to take me by his house tomorrow."

Mama just stares back at me and her lips quiver. A glitter of tears blind her eyes.

***

I wake early and unravel from the covers. My eyes are still closed, but I feel a warm tingling from my stomach that moves all the way up to my head, and I press my lips back when I think about the one hundred dollar prize that me and Simonton won. I can't wait to see Willie's face when I tell him all about what happened at the meeting last night.

I dress quickly, brush my teeth and wash my face, then go to the kitchen. Mama is preparing breakfast, moving from the cupboard to the table, and I hear the clinkering sounds of silverware hitting the wooden table.

"Good morning, Mama."

"Hey baby. Get some good sleep?"

"Yes, ma'am," I say, allowing my smile to beam more than normal. "One of the best ever. Couldn't stop thinking about last night. Did you see all them people there?"

Mama sits at the table and sips from her coffee cup. "That was way more people than I expected," she says, then allows the interior of her hands to grace the rim of the coffee cup. I want you to know, I am so proud of you, Sol. What a blessing for you."

"Thank you, Mama." I let out a light gasp and end it with a sweeping smile. "It makes me happy."

Mama taps the top of the cup with her fingertips, and her eyes begin to gloss. "Look. Um, Charlie will be here in a few minutes."

"Yes. I cain't wait. He gon' take me to Willie's house."

Mama gives me a slow nod. "Yeah, I'm going with you," she

whispers.

Charlie's truck horn is loud. I run out the door and sprint to him. "You ready?"

"Yep," Charlie says, from inside of the vehicle, "let's go." Mama closes the front door and gets into the truck.

"Morning, Charlie."

"Hey, sis."

Charlie's mood is somber, he stares through the windshield and never once allows his eyes to gaze out of the window.

We turn into Willie's yard. I hear Redbone and Bluetick howl from a good distance. My eyes spread as wide as they can and heat radiates in my chest. Charlie stops the truck. Mama pushes the door open and gets out. I whizz by her and run to the porch.

"Willie," I yell, "look what we won." *He's not on the porch.*

I turn my head and see his truck parked in front of the house. Redbone and Bluetick nibble and sniff around my feet. "Where Willie at?" Both dogs moan. Redbone lets off a light bark. I glance back at Mama and Charlie. Charlie leans against the truck and puffs on a cigarette. He says something to Mama, and she takes a slow pace towards me.

"Where Willie at, Mama?" I say, with my voice dropping sharply in mid-sentence. Mama's lips curl and her eyes flicker as she walks directly to me with her arms stretched out in front of her. "No, mama."

"Sol, comere." Mama grabs my arms.

"No, mama." I jerk away. "Where he at, Mama?" I scream.

"Sol." Mama reaches for my arms again, and I swipe downward and whip my shoulders away from her.

Charlie drops his head and turns away. The silence is heavy. I look back at Mama, she's speechless. My whole chest feels empty. I turn to the woods and sprint across the yard. I hear Redbone and Bluetick howling right behind me. "No!" I scream. The sound echoes throughout the woods. *Willie is dead.*

CHAPTER THIRTY

Silence fills the truck. I feel a whirlwind of emotions and every time I think about Willie, I hear his voice ringing in my head and my chest begins to swell. Mama has her arm wrapped around my shoulder during the entire ride, and when we get back home, I shut the door on Charlie's truck and open the tailgate for Redbone and Bluetick. They jump off the truck and lower their butts to the ground waiting for me to give them instructions.

"Comere," I say, then head to the barn. "Won't y'all go in here with Simonton and spend some time with him. I open the gate and the two dogs run in and go directly to Simonton's stall and start sniffing through the gaps in the boards. Simonton is happy to see them. He wags his tail and stands for the first time since the attack. "Sit down, boy. You cain't be getting too excited now." I put Redbone and Bluetick in Thunder's stall and give them food and water.

I walk to the woods with my head buried deep into my chest. I sit under a tree and listen to the sounds of nature all around me. I struggle to block images of Willie and his voice out of my mind. I give in after a moment and allow them to come through unfiltered.

I'm gon' miss him. I stand and dust off my pants. Willie always talked about being free in the woods, and I feel his spirit right here with me. *I never got a chance to tell him I love him.*

"I love you, Willie," I whisper to myself.

Mama and Charlie sit on chairs in front of the house. I walk across the yard, and when Mama sees me, she raises her chin.

"You okay, nephew?" Charlie asks.

"I'm okay," I mumble back to him.

"Have a seat, baby," Mama says, with her voice cracking. Her eyes are red, and she looks exhausted.

Charlie scoots forward in his chair. "I gotta few things to talk to you about."

"Okay." I take a seat and lean back.

Charlie hesitates, then begins, "Willie knew he had been sick. It's been going on for a long time. That cough never went away. It just kept nagging at 'im. Ole Willie is just like many old folk 'round here. When we get old, our bodies just start withering away. Hell, when his wife died, Willie didn't do much. He just...sat around that house there and spent time with his dogs."

"That's been a long time," Mama adds.

Charlie points at me. "Then, you came along with that dog, and it seem like Willie had something to get excited about."

"Did he ever say anything about it?" I ask.

"Oh yeah. See, Willie went to Tuskegee to get into being a

animal doctor. That's how he learned so much about dogs and stuff. After a few years up there, he came back home 'cause he had to work in the fields to help his mama nem."

"He definitely knew a lot about it," Mama says.

"Why he never say nothing about it?"

Charlie grins. "See, he wasn't a person who put all his business out there. He kept to hisself and knew what he wanted out of life. Him and Etta Mae neva had no kids so all he paid much attention to was his property and them dogs—that's it."

I drop my chin, trying to process what Charlie is sharing with us. "So, he don't have no other close family?"

"We it. He wanted to get out there to see you get that award, but when I came by to pick him up yesterday, he wasn't answering the door. So, I went on in and saw him right there in the hallway. He musta had a heart attack or something."

"My God," Mama says.

"He knew he was in bad shape. He came to my house right after he fixed Simonton on up, and we had a long talk. He gave me a will and asked me to file it at the county office."

"A will?" Mama asks.

"Yeah. He want Sol to get everything he had. The property, his truck, the dogs..." My vision blurs, and I can't hold back the emotion stirring in my chest. Tears rush down my face.

Mama reaches over and pats me on the back. "It's gon' be okay."

"He said, either give everything to Sol or donate it to the church."

When Charlie leaves, I go into my bedroom and pray. I think about how much Willie meant to me. "Dear Lord, please bless Willie.

SOL & SIMONTON

I know he's in Heaven right now looking down on me, Simonton, Redbone, and Bluetick. I will take care of them and make sure I keep talking to them about you. I love you, Willie."

Peace moves across my body and I smile, thinking about how much I learned from Willie.

***

It takes everything in me to not cry on the day of the funeral. Mama purchased me a new black suit, and Uncle Charlie cut my hair so that I can look nice for the service. I stand in the bathroom mirror fumbling with the tie that's lined under my collar and that I somehow got tied into a knot in the front.

"Awe sha, now," Mama says, walking by and stopping to observe me, "my son looking so handsome. You look like a businessman." Mama has on a long black dress with a big, stylish black hat that looks more like a crown. She has on deep red lipstick and there's a lightly coated layer of makeup on her cheeks.

"You look beautiful, Mama," I say, gleaming with a big smile.

"Why, thank you, son." Mama steps closer. "Lemme fix this. Looks like you got this thing in a knot." Mama flips the tie, moves her fingers quickly, and tucks the edge between the front base. "There you go." She pulls the back of the tie down while pulling the front up. "Now, that's how it's supposed to look. Just like that."

Mama glances at her watch, then lets her eyes connect with mine. "You okay?" she asks.

"Yes, ma'am. I'ma be okay," I say, trying to suppress my emotions.

The church parking lot is full of cars. Black suits and long black dresses move to the entrance of the church. The atmosphere is gloomy.

Why did God take Willie away?

We enter the main entrance and there are few seats available.

"Why don't y'all go on and sit up there. I'a stay back here," Charlie says. Mama and I wait for our turn to be seated by the usher. He holds out the palm of his hand and smiles. Mama and I follow his lead.

The *Amazing Grace* solo nearly brings tears to my eyes. I fight it off, keeping images of Willie out of my mind. Pastor Williams approaches the podium. He delivers a powerful eulogy on Willie and shares things about Willie's early childhood—things I didn't know about him. Pastor keeps sharing how good things were for Willie as a child, but he never spoke on the recent events in Willie's life.

Several speakers share their own personal experiences with Willie. Pastor Williams interrupts the last speaker. "I wanna thank everyone for your kind words and expressions for our brother, who, on this day, is already rejoicing with our Lord. So, I'm gon' need everyone to take a seat. I say to each one of you, there will be a day when we all must return to the dust from which we came."

"Well..." is chorused by several mourners.

"We all must follow this path—ain't no changing the course. 'Cause, only one has risen from where we must go. So, as we conclude this ceremony for our brother in Christ. We must..."

I stand. Pastor Williams shifts his eye on me, and everyone in the church looks directly at me. I turn and see the confused eyes. Mama reaches her hand up my arm. "Sol. You okay?" she whispers.

I turn and look down at Mama, who is still seated. "I'm okay, Mama." I glance back at Pastor Williams. "I have something to say, Pastor." Pastor stares for a moment, then twists his arm to view his wristwatch. "Okay, c'mon up." I scoot around several knees and walk to the podium. I have never seen so many people in one place at the same time. I see Mama and I give her a smile. She smiles back with a slight nod.

I feel sweat around my collar and want to loosen my tie, but I'm too scared to make a move. I clear my throat and hesitate. "I...I wanted to come up here and talk about somebody who was really important to me. He..."

"It's okay, baby," Mama says.

I chuckle. "He was more than a cousin to me. He taught me a lot. Not like the stuff you learn in a book, but the stuff that helps you live. I'ma miss 'im. When I'm in the woods, I'ma always think about Willie. He told me, *life is like chess board.* I remember just like he told me yesterday. There are many pieces on a chess board, but it's important to know whose board you playing on." I look up at the ceiling. "I'm not gon' ever forget that Willie. I love you." The crowd cheers. I walk out of the side door of the church and take a seat on the brick steps. Movery and Johnny exit the door right after me, and sit next to me.

"I'm sorry, Sol," Movery says. "I hate that he died. But he was a good person. And that's what you have to remember."

"Thank you, Mo."

Johnny adds, "Yeah. I'm sorry to hear that too, Sol." It seem like he was like a daddy to you."

"Thank you."

"I know I ain't seen y'all in a long time. And I hate that I been busy at home and everything," Johnny says.

"Yeah. Where you been?" Movery asks.

Johnny kicks a rock. "Just at home." I hear loud singing coming from the church.

"And I'm sorry that I ain't seen y'all in so long. I been messing with these dogs so long..." I say.

"Yeah. And you a hero now," Johnny says with a giggle.

"I'm not no hero." We all laugh. "Where you get this stuff from?"

"No, really. You might grow up to be like a superhero and save the planet from your plane to stop aliens from another country."

Movery chuckles, "Same on Johnny. Boy, you crazy."

Johnny smiles, then it turns quickly into a blank face. "Look, I wanted to tell y'all we moving again tomorrow."

"Moving? Tomorrow?" Movery asks.

"Yeah. Seems like every few years we settled and we gotta move again. The owners of the house said we gotta be out. My mama asked if he could wait 'til after the funeral and he said yes. But now we gotta go."

"Where y'all going?" I ask.

"I dunno. My mama said we might go live with her auntie in Dayton." I drop my head.

"Naw, y'all comere," Movery says. She grabs my hand and interlocks my fingers with hers. She does the same with Johnny, and we stand in a small circle. "We not gon' let nothin' stop us from believing in God."

"But we leaving tomorrow. How he gon'..."

"Shut up Johnny," Movery snaps.

"See, why you always got somethin' to say?" Johnny asks.

"'Cause you always talkin' 'bout what's not gon' happen."

"Whatchu mean?" Johnny says. "I told you we gotta leave tomorrow."

"Where's your faith?" Movery's face is serious. She moves her eyes from Johnny to me, and back to Johnny. She squeezes my hand tighter. "Now, we gon' pray for Willie, and we gon' pray that Johnny and his family get to stay here."

"Why you squeezing my hand so tight?" Johnny whines.

"Boy, you ain't gotta bit of sense," she says, "now, close your eyes and shut up while I pray."

I didn't realize how much I missed them. Though my eyes appear to be closed, I can see through my eyelashes. I feel Movery's passion every time she emphasizes a point. She squeezes my hand tighter and speaks about our faith in God. I open my eyes slightly, and Johnny is quiet and attentive.

I hear the backdoors of the church opening. Just then, Movery closes the prayer and we huddle.

"I love y'all," Johnny says.

"Love you too," Movery and I chorus.

CHAPTER THIRTY-ONE

It is the beginning of another sunny summer in 1948. The years rolled by quickly for me and Mama. Many blessings and few troubles came our way, but we have each other, and it is everything that matters to the two of us.

The house still looks the same. The roofing sheets are still corroded, and it is still evident some have been replaced over the years, as they stand out as a faded rust color in the midst of the brown. The house still has its old, rustic charm which has been weathered by the years, but the windows have been replaced.

The front yard is covered with lush grass like tiles on a floor and run all the way to the edge of the woods where the woodland canopy blocks the blue sky, and the trees bloom full and lovely with leaves.

SOL & SIMONTON

The small garden behind the barn is overgrown with vibrant wildflowers with the red sepals beautifully punctuating the green and white stalks and pollen, as butterflies flutter delicately over the nectars.

The other side of the barn bears freshly cut wood planks and two new horses stand stoutly in their stable. I built a chicken coop and had to double its size, and it's full of chicks, and bags of hay stalked, all signs of the improved life on the little farm on the edge of Sumerville, owned by the Cannings.

The one-hundred-dollar prize was only the first in a string of fortunes and blessings that came along before the end of that year. The house debt was paid off the following week, and just a month after the coonhound contest, the Washingtons rewarded Mama for her years of service to their family and gave her a bull and a cow. The two animals lay on the land behind the house, a portion that had always belonged to the family but had become wooded with weeds and short trees since it was abandoned.

I look at the house that I called home for the past seventeen years of my life, and I feel nostalgia sweep through me. Even at seventeen, I still feel a deep connection to my mother, the one parent who I have known all my life. And I know Mama loves me dearly too, even though it's hard for her to say it.

I pull a huge bag over my back and take slow steps off the porch. Mama sits in the gray rocking chair on the front porch and looks up at me from the Bible in her hands. She pulls the reading glasses from her face and smiles. "You ready?" she asks.

I nod solemnly, smiling back. "Yes, ma'am."

"Hope you've got everything packed."

"I do, mama," I answer, "and I checked two times."

Mama smiles. "So, my boy wanna fly one of them planes in the sky, huh?"

I turn back to Mama. "Yes, ma'am. I'ma be flying one of them planes."

Mama drops her Bible on her lap, and when she opens her hand, I see a watch cupped in her palm.

"I wantchu to have this," Mama says. "It's yours now."

I take a close look at the watch. "Wow. Where did you get this from?"

"It was your grandfather's. He gave it to Charlie when he became a young man, and Charlie had it all these years."

"Where Charlie anyway? Ain't he suppose to be here?"

"Well, you know how he is. He ain't one to get emotional. Say he can't stomach seeing you leave."

"He said he was coming by though," I say.

"Well, he stopped by yesterday when you was at the sto'. I bet he was watching you too. Making sure you didn't see 'im. He came by and dropped the watch off 'cause he wantchu to have it."

I bow and smile as I receive the watch. It's heavier than I expected. "Thank you, mama." I hold it in the palm of my hand and close on it tightly, thinking of my uncle and all the great times we had over the years. I drop the watch into the pocket of my trousers.

I heave the bag from my back and let it fall to the ground. "I have something for you too, mama." I unzip one of the side pockets on the bag.

I pull out a necklace and untangle it. It glitters, and I see Mama's smile spread fast across her face. "It is beautiful, isn't it?" I smile and step back onto the porch. "I bought for you." I place the necklace into her palm and close her hand against it. The necklace is silvery in color and has a tiny cross as its pendant.

"Where did you get that much money from, boy?" Mama's eyes widen again as she holds it up, and the silver sparkles in the brightness of the day.

"I been working hard, mama," I tell her and laugh softly. "It's just something for you to remember me by, mama. That's all."

Mama tilts her head up and her eyes well. "Thank you, son," she says, as she unhooks the necklace and loops it around her neck. "Comere and help me." I hop up the steps and secure the necklace around her neck.

I clap. "It looks perfect mama. You look beautiful." I smile at Mama and stare until she turns her face in embarrassment.

"Who you kidding, boy?" Mama laughs and blushes. *And what I'm saying is the truth.* The silvery chain around Mama's neck matches her eye color perfectly, and it blends with the few patches of grey that have started to show in the roots of her hairline. "You better go now. The train will leave soon."

"Yes ma'am," I say. I pick up my bag from the porch, turn to Simonton, and smile.

He's sprawled on the front porch, just beside Mama's chair and watching every move me and Mama make. I look down at Simonton and frown playfully. "Old boy, you not gon' say goodbye?"

Simonton raises his head and tries to stand, but the old, fractured bone in his right forelimb makes him falter and he drops back onto the floor. The permanent injury he suffered from the wild boar attack is still evident and the slant line that runs down his face formed a scar, a mark of his sheer bravery.

I kneel beside him and smile into his face. "You all right, old boy. You all right." I run my hand through the hair on top of his head the way I had always done since Simonton was just a puppy, and he twists his neck and laps at my fingers.

Mama and I both laugh, and Simonton wags his tail across the porch as he sits up and stares back at me.

"I'ma be gon' for a while, boy," I inform Simonton. "You will have to take care of Mama and the farm for me. You my best friend in the world, and I trust you to protect Mama." My voice drops to a mere whisper, and I feel tightness in my throat. "I'm going to the Navy, boy. And when I get back, I'ma tell you stories from all around the country and the world." A tear falls from my eyes. Simonton moans. "I promise." I kiss Simonton on the center of his head.

I stand, and Mama stands too and smiles sadly. We hug briefly and drop our hands to our sides. There are no more words left to say.

Mama pulls out a neat, white envelope from her shirt pocket. "Take this." She hands me the small envelope.

I look at Mama with questions in my eyes. "What's this, mama? Hope it's not money 'cause I got enough."

Mama shakes her head and smiles. "It is a letter, son. You can open it and read it when you get on the train."

"Okay, mama," I say, slipping the envelope into my shirt pocket. "See you later, mama. I'ma write you."

Mama presses her lips back and swallows. "I love you, Sol."

I reach forward and hug her one last time. "I love you too, mama."

I turn and take a last glance at the farm, then look back at the porch. "Simonton, old boy." Simonton lifts his head. I point to the barn. "Don't forget to protect them chickens too. And keep them boars out the yard." Simonton lets off a nice howl as if he understands the charge, and I walk toward the road.

A blue truck pulls into the yard and slows. I hoist my bag into the back of the truck. Movery exits the truck. "Hi, Miss Katherine." She smiles and waves her arm high.

"Hey, Movery. How you doing, doll?"

"Fine," Movery yells back.

"Y'all better get on up that road befo' he miss that train."

"We will."

I hug Movery and give her a light kiss on the cheek.

The ride to the train station is quiet. Every few minutes, Movery glances at me and smiles. The trees are both euphoric and eerie to me. I watch them pass by. Memories of walking down these same roads and going on adventures through the woods create butterflies in the pit of his stomach.

"Aye, stop by Willie house."

Wrinkles quickly form on Movery's forehead. "We gon' be late, Sol. You know you can't be late to the station."

"It'll only be a minute." Movery lowers her eyelids, grips the steering wheel, and snaps her head back on the road. *She's mad, and I know it. It's actually kinda cute to me.* My lips move back and transform into a smile.

We pull up to Willie's house. Johnny is in the yard playing with Redbone and Bluetick.

"Now, you know we can't be long, Sol. Two minutes, that's it," Movery says, with an elevated tone.

Johnny turns and waves when he sees us, smiling and walking to the truck.

"Johnny," I yell out of the window, dragging his name longer than I need to. I hear the heavy clumps of Johnny footsteps over the gravel and his smile grows as he gets closer to the truck.

"Aye, Sol. Look man, I got these dogs here. I'ma take care of 'em and make sure they eat right, and we gon' get on some coons when the season come around," he says, then places his palms on the interior of the door window. "When you come back, we gon' all get together and eat real good."

I feel swelling in my chest, and I dip my head to hold back the tears. *I can't cry in front of Johnny.* "That's right. We gon' all get together," I say.

"You see that, Mo?" Johnny chuckles. "He was about to cry." Movery rubs my shoulder.

"Ain't nobody about to cry, man."

"Yes, you was. Didn't he Mo?" Movery eyes fill with tears and she wipes them with a napkin.

"It's time to go," she whispers.

I raise my chin. "Y'all take care now. Okay, Johnny?"

Johnny gets quiet. "Yeah. We gon' be okay," he says. "My mama been thanking the Lord ever since you let us live here." Johnny dips his head momentarily, then raises his chin. We shake hands and end it with a snap of our fingers. Movery pulls off. Johnny stands and raises his hand slowly.

The train station is full of people from all around the area and nearby towns who have come to bid farewell to their folks. The train is scheduled to depart by noon, and the sun is shining fiercely, painting the sky a faint blue with brilliant radiance.

The air smells of smoke and tastes of dust as the train blasts its whistle and the engine starts, but the grins and happiness on the faces of the families make the atmosphere lively. A mother wails as she stands beside one of the train windows.

Movery walks me to the gate. She interlocks her fingers with mine and grips tightly. I stop before going through the gate and drop my bag.

"Okay. I think this is where I gotta say goodbye," I say, grabbing both of her hands and pulling her close to me.

Movery pauses and looks into my eyes. A tear falls and she wipes her face. "I'ma miss you, Sol."

"I'ma miss you too, Mo'."

"You remember that day when I came to your house with my daddy?"

I smile. "Yeah. I remember that day."

"Do you remember when you held me? I was emotional and crying and going crazy because I didn't know where my brother was."

"Yeah. Memories..."

"Well, that's when I knew you were special. And to this day, I love you for that. I don't want to let you go, Sol."

"Hey, hey...it's okay. I'm not leaving forever. I love you Mo'. And there's nothing more in life I want than to come back here after I serve and make you my wife."

Movery's eyes glisten. I reach into my shirt pocket and pull out a ring. "I want you to take this ring and promise to keep me dear to your heart. Promise that when I come back, you will be my wife." I slip the ring on Movery's finger. Movery bursts with tears of joy. We kiss.

The train attendant stands near the train's door. "Last call to Cleveland."

Movery touches the ring on her finger and struggles to hold her emotion. "You can't miss it, Sol. Write me soon."

"I will."

I stare deeply into her eyes. Movery leaps into my arms and grips my neck tightly. "I love you," she says.

"I love you too."

I move swiftly onto the train. Once in, I look out of the window and see Movery waving and blowing kisses until she is no longer in view.

CHAPTER THIRTY-TWO

I take a seat in the back of the train. I had packed a few biscuits and honey and knew I would chow down on them as soon as the ride started. The image of Movery waving at me keeps replaying in my head. *I wonder if she's thinking of me at this very moment.*

For the last six years, she has been my best friend, the one who knows all my secrets, the one who was there through all my pains and troubles, and the one I eventually grew to love, not only as a friend, but as the girl of my dreams. I smile sadly and think about Mama living alone in the house. I have never been away from her, and I wonder how she will cope. I reach into my breast pocket and take out the envelope Mama gave me. I open it carefully and pull out the letter.

I read the words on the envelope, "To Sol, my dear son." I

smile at those rare words. My mother doesn't write often, but her handwriting is artistic and beautiful. I settle myself into my seat beside the window, unfold the letter, and read it:

Dear Son,

I am writing this letter with both pride and love. I have watched you grow from a little baby to a kid, and to a young boy. Now that you are a man, I am proud of who you are. And I cannot ask for anything better from God.

I know I have not been able to give you everything you ever wanted, but I hope you know I was always happy to be your mama. And I am sorry for not being able to provide for everything you need. I am sorry that you didn't get many presents during all them Christmases, and I am sorry you didn't get any of them nice clothes you saw other boys have.

The things I wanted to give you in life, I could not give them to you. But I am grateful that we always had a house over our heads, and we always had each other.

I am not perfect. No one is perfect, but I hope you know I always loved you, and I will always love you. Sol, I know you always wanted to meet your father. I never wanted to keep him away from you, I just don't know where he is. I hope that one day you can meet him. I tried to find him.

I want you to fly high in the sky like you always said. Me and ole Simonton will be right here looking in the sky waiting for you to fly over the house.

Yours truly,
Mama

Made in the USA
Columbia, SC
09 October 2020